"Shall we dance?" Rafe asked

Rafe took Bri's hand and pulled her to her feet before she could renege. "We have the entire evening to convince your feet to cooperate."

This time when he put his arms around her she was much more relaxed. He held her close, the welcome feel of her breasts pressed to his chest making him question his sanity. What spell had this woman cast on him?

"You are no novice at dancing. You move like a gentle wind."

A misstep landed her on his right foot. "Thank you for breaking my concentration," Bri said.

"There is no need to concentrate. Just follow me. I will not lead you astray."

"And what if I don't have such a good partner next Saturday?"

The sudden thought of her in another man's arms made him crazy. "I will be there to rescue you."

"I don't need a chaperone."

He shrugged and urged her to lay her head on his shoulder. Her face was too close, her full pink lips too tempting. The desire to kiss her battled his common sense. "It is merely an excuse."

She drew her head back again to look at him. "An excuse for what?"

"To be with you."

Dear Reader,

It's hot outside. So why not slip into something more comfortable, like a delicious Harlequin American Romance novel? This month's selections are guaranteed to take your mind off the weather and put it to something much more interesting.

We start things off with Debbi Rawlins's *By the Sheikh's Command*, the final installment of the very popular BRIDES OF THE DESERT ROSE series. Our bachelor prince finally meets his match in a virginal beauty who turns the tables on him in a most delightful way. Rising star Kara Lennox begins a new family-connected miniseries, HOW TO MARRY A HARDISON, and these sexy Texas bachelors will make your toes tingle. You'll meet the first Hardison brother in *Vixen in Disguise*—a story with a surprising twist.

The talented Debra Webb makes a return engagement to Harlequin American Romance this month with *The Marriage Prescription*, a very emotional story involving characters you've met in her incredibly popular COLBY AGENCY series from Harlequin Intrigue. Also back this month is Leah Vale with *The Rich Girl Goes Wild*, a not-to-be-missed billionaire-in-disguise story.

Here's hoping you enjoy all we have to offer this month at Harlequin American Romance. And be sure to stop by next month when Cathy Gillen Thacker launches her brand-new family saga, THE DEVERAUX LEGACY.

Best,

Melissa Jeglinski
Associate Senior Editor
Harlequin American Romance

BY THE SHEIKH'S COMMAND

Debbi Rawlins

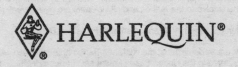

HARLEQUIN®

TORONTO • NEW YORK • LONDON
AMSTERDAM • PARIS • SYDNEY • HAMBURG
STOCKHOLM • ATHENS • TOKYO • MILAN • MADRID
PRAGUE • WARSAW • BUDAPEST • AUCKLAND

Special thanks and acknowledgment are given to
Debbi Rawlins for her contribution to the
BRIDES OF THE DESERT ROSE series.

This book is for Tina Colombo.
Thank you for your understanding and patience
and wonderful editing. It's a joy to work with you.

ISBN 0-373-16933-7

BY THE SHEIKH'S COMMAND

Copyright © 2002 by Harlequin Books S.A.

Visit us at www.eHarlequin.com

Printed in U.S.A.

ABOUT THE AUTHOR

Debbi Rawlins currently resides with her husband and dog in Las Vegas, Nevada. A native of Hawaii, she married on Maui and has since lived in Cincinnati, Chicago, Tulsa, Houston, Detroit and Durham, North Carolina, during the past twenty years. Now that she's had enough of the gypsy life, it'll take a crane, a bulldozer and a forklift to get her out of her new home. Good thing she doesn't like to gamble. Except maybe on romance.

Books by Debbi Rawlins

Don't miss any of our special offers. Write to us at the following address for information on our newest releases.

Harlequin Reader Service
U.S.: 3010 Walden Ave., P.O. Box 1325, Buffalo, NY 14269
Canadian: P.O. Box 609, Fort Erie, Ont. L2A 5X3

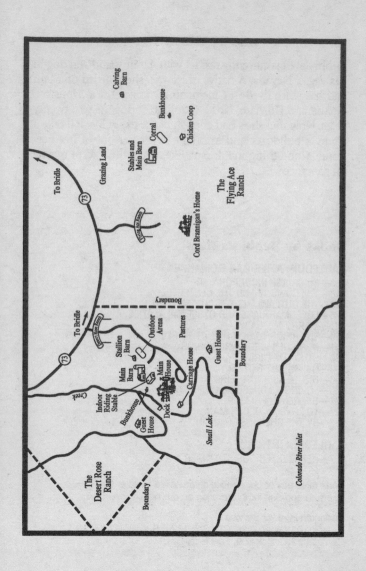

Chapter One

Brianna Taylor saw him standing in the shadows, and held her breath. She would never have come to the barn if she had known Sheikh Rafe Bahram would be there. In fact, she wouldn't have come at all.

Afraid to exhale, she stood, frozen, watching him, curious as to what he was doing. Unlike the angry man who'd arrived over a week ago, he seemed calm and at peace now. His dark head bowed forward, he murmured something she was too far away to hear. The tone reached her, though, low, soothing, hypnotic, as if he were whispering words of love to a woman.

The idea startled her. No one else was in the barn. Besides, with Allie gone, Bri was the only woman on the ranch. He spoke again and then ducked out of view. Fascinated, she took an involuntary step forward, and then abruptly realized he was talking to Magic Carpet, the Flying Ace's newest colt, born only two weeks ago.

Luckily, Rafe hadn't seen her. It wasn't too late to back out and run to the house. No one was there. Cord and Rafe's sister, Allie, had left for their honeymoon. The reminder that her brother now had a wife, someone else to share his life, dealt a fresh blow of grief and her steps faltered.

Not that she wasn't happy for him. She truly was thrilled that he'd found someone so perfect for him like Allie, but it had been only a year since Bri had found Cord, only a year of having someone genuinely care about her and not consider her existence a burden to the modern world.

Rafe's head came up again and she stopped, fearing any movement would attract his attention. He started to turn toward her and, without another thought, she dropped to the ground in a crouched position.

Immediately she regretted it.

How foolish. She could have waved and then walked out. It wasn't as if she'd been spying on him. But it was too late and all she could hope for...

"What are you doing?"

The nearness of Rafe's husky, accented voice startled her. He stood only a foot away. She looked up into his concerned dark eyes, lost her balance and landed on her fanny on the hard floor.

"Brianna." He bent over to take her elbow, but she evaded him.

Humiliation stung her cheeks. "I'm looking for my earring. I lost it." He continued to stare at her with unnerving intensity. Maybe because she never wore earrings. She was too chicken to get her ears pierced. She averted her gaze and focused on the hay-littered floor. "I lost it yesterday."

"Yesterday?"

She nodded without looking up and sifted through the hay.

"In this exact spot?"

She nodded again, and then the amusement in his voice registered, and she looked up. A ghost of a smile played at the corners of his mouth. She was fairly certain she hadn't seen him smile before.

"Well, not in this exact spot. If I knew that, then it wouldn't be lost, would it?" She lowered her gaze again when she realized how prickly she sounded.

He laughed softly and crouched beside her. "I will help you search."

"No." She swallowed when his knee brushed her thigh. "I'm fine. Really."

She'd never been this close to him. Once they'd sat opposite each other across the dinner table, but he'd been in an awful mood, his face darkened by a scowl. He'd come to Bridle to take his sister back to their home in Munir but found out Allie and Cord were getting married. That Allie had tricked him by switching places with her maid and remaining behind in Texas still amazed Brianna. Allie was her new hero. Bri would never have had the nerve.

"Of course you are, but two of us searching would be better, would it not?"

"I'm sure you have more important things to do," she muttered as she stared down at the clumps of straw she'd formed.

"What could be more important than helping a lady in distress?"

At the amusement in his voice, she looked up and

their eyes met in challenge. "Where I come from, losing an earring is hardly a disaster."

"Where I come from, a lady sometimes loses something to gain a man's attention. Perhaps with the intent of initiating a…friendship."

Brianna stared back in disbelief. Her mouth opened, but nothing came out. And then finally she said, "That's stupid."

He smiled, taking some of the sting out of her less-than-profound comment. "I agree."

"You don't do that enough."

"Do what?"

She blinked, stunned that she'd said that out loud. "Never mind."

"I would like to hear this."

"It's no big deal." She shrugged and looked away. "You don't smile enough."

"Ah." If he was surprised at her observation, he hid it well. "Why do you prefer that I smile?"

"I don't," she said quickly. "I just don't want you to still be angry that Allie tricked you. You have to see how happy she is, how madly in love she and Cord are." She sighed. "Having someone love you that much is like—" She stopped, mortification stinging her cheeks.

"Go on. What is it like?"

"I was talking about Allie and Cord." Oh, God, she wanted to stand up and run as fast as she could. To the lake at the foot of the Desert Rose, where no one bothered her, where she could sit and stare at the peaceful water and make believe life was perfect.

"Yes, but you seem to have strong feelings about—"

"Oh, here's my gold hoop." She fisted her hand around some hay and pretended to stuff the imaginary earring into her jeans pocket. Her face flamed with the lie, but she couldn't do much about it but turn away as she got to her feet. "Well, see you later."

"Wait." Rising with her, he touched her arm and she froze. "You seem upset. Why?"

She refused to meet his gaze. "I'm not."

"Then look at me."

She haltingly obeyed. The way he stared silently at her made her nervous, as if he were studying a painting. More likely he stared because her nose was a little crooked from a childhood fall. "What?"

"You have extraordinary eyes."

She blinked. "No, I don't."

His lips curved again.

She hunched her shoulders, wishing she could be someone else. Just this once. Someone beautiful and sophisticated, who said and did all the right things. "I really have to go."

"First, tell me." His gaze narrowed in concern. "Why does it bother you that I will be staying with you in Cord and Aliah's absence?"

The reminder of her brother's overprotective stubborn streak made her blood boil. "I don't need looking after, and he had no business asking you to stick around."

"That is not why I am staying."

"Don't try and cover up for him. I heard him ask you, remember?"

Rafe moved his broad shoulders in a slow shrug. "I believe he was teasing you. He knows the foal I have purchased from the Colemans of the Desert Rose Ranch should be born within a week, and that I wished to be present for the birth."

Bri forced herself to meet his dark, steady gaze. He looked so darn sincere, yet she knew her brother, and she doubted very much that Cord had been teasing. When Rafe said nothing more, she asked, "How long will you be here?"

"At least until the foal is born."

"Don't you have to get back to Munir?"

"You sound as if you wish to get rid of me."

She blushed again. Darn it. "I thought you were a busy man. Allie said you—" She cut herself off and gritted her teeth.

"What did my sister say?"

"Nothing important." She dusted her hands together. "I need to go see about supper."

"Wait, Brianna."

She'd never liked her name. Taunted as a child by Jenny Thomas and other girls with nice normal names, she'd even hated it for a while. But the husky way Rafe said it erased all those hurtful years in an instant.

He gazed down at her in that intense unnerving way of his, and she had little choice but to hear him out.

"I hope you do not have a problem with us being alone in the house while your brother is away."

"Of course not." She was getting to be way too

good a liar. Her aunt Elaine would have washed her mouth out with soap.

"If so, I can arrange to stay in Bridle."

Confused, she studied him for a moment. Was he right about Cord only teasing her? Otherwise, Rafe wouldn't offer to stay in town. "What about the Desert Rose?"

In response to her bluff, his right eyebrow went up. "I am making you uncomfortable?"

"Don't be silly. It's not that I don't want you here—" Her tongue got tied and she stumbled over her words. "I just thought that since you want to be there for the foal's birth…" At the telling amusement on his face, she groaned inwardly. "I really need to go see about supper."

"Aliah did not make arrangements?"

"Why would she? They left early yesterday." Bri groaned out loud this time. "Unless she ordered pizza."

"Pizza?" He smiled "Ah, yes. While I was at the university, it was a favorite dish of many of the students."

"In Munir?"

"No, Harvard."

"You went to Harvard? Here, in the United States?"

His eyebrows rose. "Why do you find that so difficult to believe?"

"I don't know. I—" She shrugged. "I knew that Allie had a British tutor. I guess I assumed—I don't know."

"It is different for women in our country."

"I guess that's why Allie ran away." Her hand flew to her mouth. Allie had complained about women being nonentities, merely a man's accessory. "I'm sorry. I didn't mean to—I'd better go."

His expression tightened. "I am not ignorant of my country's archaic attitudes or shortcomings. Now, I've detained you long enough. Please excuse me."

Bri kept her mouth shut as he strolled back toward Magic Carpet's stall. She hadn't meant to offend him. Allie had wonderful things to say about her brother. She'd felt badly about tricking him into offering her maid to Cord when he'd rescued the woman from a runaway horse. But secretly trading places with the maid and staying behind in America was the only way Allie could get out from beneath the royal thumb.

Rafe wasn't like their parents, Allie had confided, or the rest of the royals. He respected a woman's right to independence and strongly advocated modernizing their country even though it was an unpopular political position.

Bri didn't understand any of it, but she liked and respected Allie. So if Allie thought her brother was honorable it was enough for Bri. She was glad, too. Men as gorgeous and as powerful as Rafe weren't always nice, in Bri's limited experience. Not that she'd ever met a sheikh before.

Or anyone like Rafe. It didn't matter that she'd hardly spoken to him. Just looking at him made her skin tingle and caused a flutter in her tummy. Watching him wasn't like watching the ranch hands, not even the new guy Chuck, and he was pretty cute with his sandy-colored hair and twinkling blue eyes.

With his midnight hair, dark seductive eyes and tall lean frame, Rafe was in a category all by himself. Taller than all the other guys on the ranch except Cord, he towered over her. At five nine, she couldn't wear high heels around most men. Which suited her fine. She'd worn heels twice at her aunt Elaine's insistence. It had been awful.

She waited until Rafe was back in Magic Carpet's stall, his back to her, before she headed out of the barn toward the house, and to Cord's study. He'd left some notes for her regarding the stock selection for next month's cattle auction and now seemed like a good time to bury herself in work.

Better that she didn't think about Rafe or that he would be sleeping only three rooms away from her for the next week. Anyway, the annual auction was important to the Flying Ace, and she wanted to do the best job possible in Cord's absence.

He'd been so good to her, going to New Hampshire to bring her back to Bridle. Although they had the same father, Bri was the bastard child, the product of a brief affair Gerald Brannigan had had with her mother in Dallas. Bri had never known him, in fact she'd barely known her mother. Aunt Elaine, her mother's older sister, had raised Bri.

None of that mattered to Cord. He'd made it clear the ranch would always be her home, as much hers as it was his. Ironically, he'd accepted her as a Brannigan much more quickly and completely than she had accepted his generosity. But day by day she'd begun to settle in and experience the wonder of belonging she'd craved her entire childhood.

That's why it chafed that Cord hadn't mentioned to her privately about extending the invitation to stay to Rafe. She wouldn't have dreamed of not consulting Cord before inviting a guest. But then again, Rafe was now Cord's brother-in-law. Of course he'd be welcome at any time.

Her pulse sped up and it had nothing to do with the fact that she had practically power walked up the slope to the house. The thought that Rafe might become a frequent visitor had sent her heart into overdrive. Not that she expected anything to happen between them. Even though Allie had teased her to watch out because Rafe had a taste for blondes. Or because he thought Bri had extraordinary eyes…

She entered through the kitchen and then detoured down the hall to her room and shut the door. She still wanted to tackle the auction paperwork this afternoon but something more pressing required her attention. The mirror over her dresser was smudged, so she wiped it with her sleeve and stared up close at her reflection.

All that stared back were plain ol' garden-variety blue eyes. A hint of green was the only thing possibly interesting about them. Which was a stretch. Especially considering that her crooked nose drew attention away from anything that might be pleasant about her face.

She peered closer. Maybe some makeup would help hide the flaw. Mascara was about all she could handle daily. Aunt Elaine didn't believe in vanity and would have taken a switch to Bri if she ever "painted her face." But Allie and Bri's friend, Jessica Coleman

Grayson, both wore makeup. That didn't make them tramps.

Sighing, Bri pulled her ponytail up and piled her hair high on top of her head, and then angled her face to get a look from either side. The style made her look slightly older, anything older than twenty-two was good.

Maybe she'd experiment later, after dinner.

Shoot! She'd forgotten about dinner. Rafe had distracted her. He was pretty darn good at doing that, all right. It would serve him right if Allie had ordered pizza for them…although that was doubtful. Allie wasn't the type to worry about anything else on the eve of her honeymoon.

Not that Bri blamed her. If she were so lucky as to find a husband who was as crazy about her as Cord was about Allie, Bri wouldn't think about much else, either. And frankly, Bri was glad Allie wasn't the domestic type or terribly organized, either. Wouldn't that create a need for Bri to stick around?

Even when their housekeeper returned, there were still household decisions to be made, the kind that Bri handled.

Sighing, she let go of her hair and the ponytail fell like a heavy rope down her back. She'd thought about cutting it, but a shorter style would require too much care. With working around the ranch, a ponytail was much easier to manage.

Assuming she'd be around much longer.

Angry with herself, she chased the hurtful thought away. Hadn't she just reasoned that she had a necessary place here? Of course, for the past week her thoughts had been bouncing back and forth like a rubber ball.

One minute she convinced herself that it would be best if she left the ranch and the newlyweds to their privacy, and in the next breath she decided Cord's marriage didn't mean she had to leave. She had a viable job at the ranch. Cord didn't like doing the bookkeeping and she did. She was darn good at it, too. The grain costs had gone down since she'd taken over and found another supplier—someone who wasn't related to the acting foreman while Manny had been away.

The best thing Aunt Elaine had ever done was encourage, no, demand, that Bri get an education. Her maiden aunt had been vocal about Bri learning to take care of herself, and not end up like her mother, Elaine's sister, who'd gotten knocked up and then abandoned her daughter to the charity of her family.

At first Bri had silently rebelled, but then she discovered that school not only got her out of the house and away from Aunt Elaine's harping, but it was fun and empowering. She'd done extremely well, making the honor roll all through high school, and then the dean's list her second and third year of college. She'd probably have made it her senior year, too, had she finished. But the lure of meeting her brother had eclipsed her need for a degree.

Her stomach growled, reminding her she really did have to think about rustling something up for dinner. Maybe sandwiches. If His Royal Highness didn't like that option, he could go to the diner in Bridle. Give the townspeople something to gawk at.

Bri smiled at the thought as she strolled into the kitchen and opened the fridge. Nothing leaped out at her. They'd finished the leftovers last night and she hadn't taken anything out of the freezer. Even the deli meat looked unappealing.

Pizza didn't sound so bad right about now. Although, since Allie had discovered the spicy pies for the first time last week, they'd had pepperoni, peppers and extra cheese four times for dinner.

She considered taking a drive into Bridle to pick one up, when she saw a folded piece of paper stuck to the side of the refrigerator under a cow magnet. Curious, she unfolded it. Cord usually left notes for her on her desk.

The message was from Allie. She had ordered their dinner to be delivered from the diner at seven. Rafe had been right. Bri frowned. The diner didn't deliver. Of course, Allie had a way of getting what she wanted. Bri needed to take lessons.

Her gaze fell on the tiny postscript at the bottom from Cord. They had decided to stop in Dallas on the way back and would be home a day later than the planned ten days.

No big deal. What was one day?

She set the note aside, a wave of melancholy overtaking her. This was yet another change in the way she and Cord had settled into life on the ranch together. In the past, he had always kept her informed of his plans, even if it was only a trip to the bank. Now he had Allie.

Bri hated the jealousy that gnawed at her, but it was there, and she would have to make peace with it.

Ignoring it would only fuel needless resentment. Cord's marriage posed no threat to her relationship with him. As he'd assured her so many times, they'd always be family.

As far as Allie having taken charge of dinner tonight, that had been a nice gesture. Really. Bri didn't have to worry about playing hostess to Rafe right off the bat. Allie had been thoughtful in eliminating that problem.

Bri got a six-pack of cola out of the pantry and put it on the fridge. So why did she feel so glum? Now she had more time to work on the auction paperwork.

She started for her office but her gaze fell on the newspaper left on the kitchen table. Ironically, it was open to the classifieds—the rental section.

Was someone trying to tell her something?

Chapter Two

Rafe stopped at the wet bar in the living room and found the bottle of scotch his new brother-in-law had left him. He poured himself a glass. Neat. No ice. Just the way he liked it. The scotch was a rare pleasure he allowed himself only when he traveled abroad. In his own country he never drank liquor. He never did anything that could be deemed inappropriate. He had too much to lose.

That's what made the purpose of this trip to Texas so ironic. The fact that he would return to Munir without his errant sister as a result of his own negligence was more inappropriate than a dozen drinks.

He downed half the glass of scotch, and then took the rest with him to the den where he could look out at the courtyard fountain. The house was quiet, although he knew Brianna was somewhere inside. From the stables he had watched her cross the lawn and enter the house less than an hour ago.

She was an amazingly graceful creature. Tall and lithe and elegant even in faded jeans. A natural beauty who was inordinately reserved. In his experience, most women who possessed such perfection flaunted their attributes, expected special treatment. Although he had not had too many exchanges with her, Brianna seemed as quiet as a little mouse.

She could have been born to royalty by the way she carried herself, but he knew better. Cord had explained a little about his sister, about her shyness, how she kept to herself, going swimming or riding when not at work on the Flying Ace's books. He was concerned about her swimming alone at a nearby lake, and Rafe had assured him he would be watchful of her.

And also discreet. Cord had immediately regretted that Brianna knew he had asked Rafe to watch over her. He smiled at the memory of her annoyed reaction when she had overheard them talking, how she had been quick to remind Cord that she was almost twenty-three and needed no supervision.

Rafe had decided to downplay his presence, allow her to think he had no interest in her whereabouts or activities. Apparently, she stayed close to the ranch, sometimes visiting friends at the Desert Rose or swimming in the lake.

Four of the five men living in the bunkhouse had been with the Brannigan family for years and did not concern Cord. The fifth one, however, a young man hired recently, showed too much interest in Brianna. Cord had not yet found it necessary to warn the man, but Rafe's instructions were to "break the guy's neck if he sniffed around Bri."

Staring out at the waning sun, Rafe smiled at Cord's choice of words and his intense protectiveness.

An unusual quality among the American men Rafe had met at Harvard or since. Women were more independent in this country—an admirable trait to be sure, but sometimes difficult for a brother to accept.

"I'm sorry. I didn't know you were in here."

At the sound of Brianna's voice, he turned to find her backing out of the room. "Is it a crime in Texas for us to be in the same room?"

Confusion flickered in her eyes at his teasing. And then she made a face. "I simply meant I didn't want to disturb you."

"Ah, I see." He gestured to a chair. "Please, sit with me."

She glanced toward the door as if seeking escape. "I'm sort of busy right now."

"Of course." He drained his scotch, and contemplated another.

Brianna stared at him. When he met her gaze, she quickly looked away, her cheeks flooding with color. "You were right about dinner. Allie ordered something. I'll let you know when it gets here."

Rafe did not know the Brannigan family history, only that Brianna had not been raised in Bridle, but had led a sheltered life in a small town in New England. Perhaps that was the reason for her shyness. Perhaps that was what intrigued him about her. "May I fix you a drink?" he asked before she could leave.

She frowned slightly.

"You are old enough?"

She gave him a scathing look. "I'm almost twenty-three."

"That old?"

The corners of her mouth twitched. "Very funny," she said, and to his satisfaction, she lowered herself to a chair. "I'll remind you that Allie and I are close in age and she's now a married woman."

His mood darkened. That was a reminder he did not need. He liked and respected Cord, but Aliah's marriage to him had caused a great deal of trouble. "Yes, but until she was married, Aliah was under my patronage."

Brianna laughed. "Patronage?"

He nodded.

"That sounds archaic."

"Perhaps, but it is Munir's custom for a brother to be responsible for his sister."

She lifted her chin. "Good thing I don't live there."

Rafe made no comment, as tempted as he was to point out that she lived under the protection of Cord, and that in many aspects their cultures were not so vastly different.

"I'm not sure I'll be here for dinner," she said after a brief silence. "I may be meeting friends in Bridle."

"All right." He did not believe her. She was testing him, seeing if he would question her. "I have some work I must do for my meeting in Dallas. I would have preferred your company, but I understand."

She seemed to relax. "I didn't say I was going for sure. In fact, no one's called yet so I probably won't." She eyed his empty glass. "I'll fix you another drink if you want."

He handed her the glass, their fingers brushing in the exchange. "The scotch, if you will. But just half. I need to keep my wits about me."

He deliberately sought her gaze, and she stiffened, her eyes growing wide. The innuendo had not been lost. But he had meant only to tease her, not frighten her. She truly was naive, a child in many ways.

Bri quickly got up. She was glad for the excuse to go to the living room for the drink. He made her so darn nervous and had her thinking all kinds of crazy thoughts. That dark sexy look he gave her made her imagination go a little nuts.

Plus, she'd heard a lot about him from Allie. He was quite a ladies' man, although Allie claimed he never took advantage of the fact that women were drawn to his looks and power. Bri didn't know what exactly it was about him, but something sure got her all hot and bothered. The feeling was both unfamiliar and a little frightening.

She wasn't worried, though. Not about his intentions. And it wasn't just because of Allie's glowing praise of her brother. Bri put more stock in the way Rafe treated Allie, in the way they interacted.

Watching Allie and Rafe say their goodbyes yesterday had made her a little wistful. The way they could give each other one look and smile in understanding, or the way he unabashedly hugged and kissed Allie. Even though Rafe still had to be hurt and angry over the way she had tricked him into leaving her in Texas, the love and acceptance he'd shown his sister warmed Bri in a way she couldn't describe. It made her like him.

But it also made her envious. Rafe and Allie had a long history together. Not like her and Cord. They'd only known each other for a short time. If she were to suddenly move back to New Hampshire, Cord would miss her, she felt sure, but it wouldn't devastate him.

She found the bottle of scotch and poured a small amount into Rafe's glass. It crossed her mind to have a little wine, but she had the auction paperwork to handle and a stack of invoices to pay and payroll to prepare and…

The truth was, she didn't trust herself to indulge in anything mind-altering. God only knew what she'd blab if she got too relaxed. She grabbed a bottle of diet cola instead and as she turned to go, nearly stepped on Mittens.

Allie's kitten let out a wail and Bri nearly dropped Rafe's drink as she jumped back. "Oh, you poor thing, I'm so sorry." Bri set the glass of scotch and bottle of cola on the bar and stooped to cuddle the kitten, but the little thing scurried out of the room.

"Are you all right?" Rafe appeared almost instantly. He grabbed her upper arms as she straightened, his concerned eyes probing hers.

"Fine." She cleared her throat. "It was Mittens. She got underfoot and we sort of scared each other."

He glanced around.

"She's probably halfway to the stables by now."

His hands tightened slightly around her arms and he studied her face with unnerving closeness.

"What?" Bri tried to take a step back.

"Have you ever been alone before?"

She laughed at the irony. "I've been alone plenty, believe me. Besides, you're here, aren't you?"

"Yes," he said so patiently it annoyed her. "And if you need anything—"

"I won't."

He nodded, but his condescending expression irked her. True, she hadn't been in charge of the ranch before, but two of the hands had been with the Flying Ace so long they didn't need her. Ty Thomas and Joe Piedmont had started right after Cord's father had bought the ranch.

Her father. The thought stopped her. Even after hearing Cord's stories and seeing all the pictures, she still couldn't think of Gerald Brannigan as her father. She did wish she had met him, though. But he'd died unaware of her existence.

"Of course, you can always call Cord on his cell phone."

She glared at Rafe. "I will not."

"Because he is on his honeymoon? Business is business. Cord understands."

"So do I. But a honeymoon is a honeymoon, and if he doesn't understand that, I'm sure Allie will help remind him."

A hint of a smile lit his face. "I am sure you are quite right. Subtlety is not my sister's strong suit."

"Subtlety has nothing to do with it. Now that they're married, priorities have changed."

"Ah." He nodded. "You are a romantic."

"No, I'm not." Why did she sound so defensive? If she were a romantic, it wouldn't be a crime. "Marriage is important."

"I agree." He gave a curt bow. "It is much like business."

That stopped her. Marriage was personal. It was about love and respect between two people who couldn't bear to live without each other. But of course Munir royalty didn't share that opinion. Allie had explained about duty to family and country coming before personal desire. Maybe having no family wasn't so bad after all.

"I see you do not agree," Rafe said when she stayed silent. "Americans do not understand. American women in particular do not—"

She put up a hand. "I wouldn't finish that thought if I were you."

"As you wish." His dark eyes watched her with such intensity it was as if he could see more than he should. "Where are you going?"

"To my office." She took the glass from the bar and handed it to him before she headed out. "I have a lot of work to do."

"Brianna. Wait."

She hesitated, but didn't actually turn around, torn between curiosity and the need to rush to the safety of her office.

"Brianna?"

Curiosity won. She turned to him.

"Will you run from me the entire week?"

AFTER DINNER, Rafe sat outside in the patio, sipping his coffee while Brianna cleaned up the kitchen. She had declined his offer to help but promised to sit with him later. But only after he had nearly badgered her into agreeing.

She was a puzzle, that one. Perhaps by the time Aliah and Cord returned, he would understand the shy blonde more. Why she blushed so easily and seemed to shrink away from attention instead of making the most of her considerable charms. She had him confused. Few people were able to do that.

"I brought you some brandy," she said as she stepped onto the patio. "Sometimes Cord has it with his coffee after dinner." She set the bottle down on the table, along with a crystal snifter.

"What about you? Will you not join me?"

She wrinkled her nose. "I don't like the stuff. It's too strong."

"I agree. Please. Sit."

A blush stole across her cheeks, and she drew in her lower lip beneath even white teeth, a nervous habit he found most appealing. "I'll stay a few minutes," she said and then sank into the chair farthest from him.

He picked up his coffee, not in the least interested in the brandy. A restless energy disturbed his equilibrium. Is that why he looked to this shy beauty for distraction?

"Well, if you don't need me anymore..."

"Why do you run from me? Has Aliah filled your head with horror stories?"

She'd started to rise, but sank back down, looking genuinely surprised. "No, of course not. She adores you. And I don't understand why you keep thinking

I'm running away. I'm not on vacation. I have work to do.''

"I have asked only for a few minutes."

She sighed. "I'm sorry. I am a little edgy. There are just so many changes around here lately…"

Rafe studied the way she anxiously smoothed back the tendrils of hair that had come loose, looking as if she wanted to get up and run as fast as she could. "Were you not in favor of the marriage?" he asked quietly.

"No. I mean, yes." She gave her head a flustered shake. "I love Allie like a sister. I'm happy for both of them."

"Yet the balance here is upset."

Her forehead creased in a frown and she shrugged.

"Brianna, I understand. I have made peace with the marriage, but still it is difficult for me to see Aliah with a husband. In fact, a near stranger. No matter my growing fondness for Cord." He had failed to take Aliah back. His people would not understand. "But she made her choice."

Curiosity lit her eyes. "I thought men in your country didn't believe in giving women a choice."

"Most don't."

"But you do."

He lifted the coffee cup to his lips. He did not wish to discuss his personal views.

"Allie said you're very modern."

"My sister talks too much." He set the cup aside. "I understand there is a lake near here?"

Brianna stiffened. "A small one."

"I would like to see it sometime."

"It's just an ordinary lake. You won't be impressed."

"My country is nearly surrounded by the Persian Gulf. The water soothes me."

"I know. Me, too, but this really is a tiny lake and you're used to an ocean."

"No matter. When you are not too busy, you will show me?"

Reluctance hunched her shoulders. "Okay."

"Tomorrow afternoon perhaps?"

Alarm darkened her eyes. "I'm not sure I'll have time."

She clearly did not want her private sanctuary invaded. Or perhaps it was his company she wished to avoid. The idea did not warm him. Women normally sought his attention.

She got to her feet and started gathering his cup and the brandy and placing them on the tray. Her hands fumbled in her haste and the idea she wanted to get away from him grew stronger.

He touched her wrist. "You seem nervous."

Her face ripened with color. "I already explained why I was edgy." Her chest rose and fell with a deep shuddering breath, and his gaze drew to her breasts.

Beneath the plain white T-shirt she wore, her nipples protruded. He dragged his gaze away, not wanting to embarrass her. And then he quickly released her, annoyed at his own physical reaction.

"D-did you want anything else?" Her lower lip quivered and she hesitated picking up the tray.

When she lowered her gaze, his own went back to her chest. Her breasts were small, the perfect size for the palm of a man's hand, her nipples lush and tempting. Desire stirred in his belly and he clenched his teeth.

Too bad she was a child. Not just because she was ten years younger than he, but her obvious lack of experience around men detracted further. Cord had warned him she was an innocent, but a brother's viewpoint was not always reliable.

Rafe mentally shook his head. Look how Aliah had fooled him. She had been sheltered, even cloistered for many of her young years, and she had turned into a hellcat nevertheless.

But he did not want to think about his sister and the predicament she had created for him. Soon enough he would have to face the royal family and admit his failure.

Brianna picked up the tray, her hands much steadier now. "I have a desk in Cord's office. I'll be in there if you need me."

"And if I need you now?"

She blinked, and visibly swallowed. "Need me?"

He smiled. "Go, Brianna. Go hide in your office."

A glint of temper flared in her eyes, but she said nothing. She gripped the tray with tight little fists and backed away from the table.

He watched her go, admiring the fit of her jeans. Normally, he preferred the soft curves and expanse of leg revealed by a dress. But the way the worn fabric clung to Brianna's backside had his body stirring again.

Disgusted with himself, he turned away and focused on the fountain. He had given Cord his word he would care for his sister. That did not include troubling her with unwanted attention.

The soothing sound of water reached his ears, and the lights lit the spray like a thousand diamonds. There was no balm for his damaged spirit like the power of water. Yes, he had wanted to know where the lake was so that he could find Brianna should she disappear. But he wanted the knowledge for himself, as well.

He had much to think about before returning to Munir. Politically, he was now vulnerable. His cousin, Asaad, would seize the opportunity to vie for the throne. Although Rafe was the rightful heir, Assad had enough bloodline and connections to persuade the royal council his agenda was better suited to Munir's interests.

While he wanted Munir to remain a monarchy, Rafe was in favor of moving toward a democracy. The people had mixed opinions. Munir subjects were accustomed to being coddled and having decisions made for them. Since the land and surrounding sea were both rich with oil, and everyone was well fed, with filled pockets, the people had little interest in change.

But some of the oil fields were drying up, and in order for the royal family to maintain their wealth, the difference in profits would come from the people. Asaad knew that as well as Rafe did, but his cousin was unwilling to sacrifice even a shadow of his assets. To that end, it was imperative he kept the people under his control, kept the country in the backward state in which it languished.

Rafe watched the water cascade from the tiled fountain and took several deep even breaths. Meditation had become as important to him as sleep. Next week in Dallas, he would need all his energy and wits about him. The largest oil lease with the Dallas-based American company was about to expire. It would be up to Rafe to negotiate the best possible deal.

Failing to bring Aliah back was serious. Failing to secure a lucrative deal would be unforgivable. Certain political suicide. Not that he was concerned. He had oil—something the Americans wanted and he knew how to do business with them. That was something he had over Asaad.

His cousin had gone to London and Paris for his education. Although from what the family had heard, he'd spent little time on his studies. Rafe had lived in the United States for six years while attending Harvard. Before that, he had had an American tutor who taught him English from the age of four. And unlike Asaad who showed open disdain for Americans, Rafe liked them. He liked the progressive way they thought, the democratic way they governed and their humanitarian concern for third-world countries.

And he liked American women. The way they dressed and smelled. He especially admired the way they spoke their minds on subjects ranging from politics to child rearing. Of course, in his country, women were not given the same freedom to be so outspoken, but then again, it had not stopped young women like Aliah.

Rafe closed his eyes at the thought of his unruly sister. He hoped she truly had found what she wanted, and this marriage was not a mere act of rebellion. He did not believe so. Not the way she and Cord looked at each other, or the laughter they shared. Rafe had never heard his sister laugh so much as he had in the past few days.

In a way, he envied her. True, the royal family and the people of Munir would not be happy, but at least her taking an American husband could be tolerated. He did not have that luxury. When he finally wedded, the bride would be well chosen according to Munir custom. The idea was a farce. Even as queen, his wife would have no power, or avenue to voice her opinions.

No matter, he would have to find a wife soon before one was selected for him. His parents reminded him often he would soon be past his prime.

Unwilling to dwell anymore on the unpleasant subject, he got up from the table and considered going for a ride to the Desert Rose. Not in the pickup truck but on one of Cord's fine stallions. Between the Desert Rose and the Flying Ace, the quality of horses they bred would warrant many more scouting trips. Already he had purchased a small herd, but there was always room in the royal stables for another fine thoroughbred.

More important, he would want to visit Aliah. Assure himself all was well with her husband and her new life in America. And of course he would be able to see Brianna.

The thought startled him. Without a doubt he found her very beautiful with her long blond hair and clear blue eyes, and her reserved demeanor was most captivating. But he had not consciously been thinking about her.

Still, she often stole into his thoughts, he realized, uneasiness crawling beneath his skin. He had to move, not sit and think. Brianna would be in her office. A trip to the Desert Rose in the moonlight would occupy him. Perhaps Mac Coleman was still in the stables so they could discuss the foal.

Rafe changed into a pair of jeans, attire to which he had become accustomed while studying at Harvard but seldom wore now. He seemed to live in ties and suits, traveling in the family jet from one meeting to another to wherever the demand for oil led him. Staying here at the Flying Ace would do him good.

He thought about stopping at Brianna's office to let her know he would be out, but then thought it better she believed he was still around the Flying Ace. Instead, he headed for the stables, enjoying the last remnants of the sunset.

He wished he could share it with Brianna.

The unexpected and intrusive thought angered him and he pushed through the stable doors.

What was it about the girl that she'd slipped into his thoughts so easily? Could it be he wanted more than to keep an eye on her?

Chapter Three

"Hey, Bri, you're looking good this morning."

She spun around with her hand to her throat. "Good grief, Chuck, you scared the living daylights out of me."

"Sorry, darlin', I sure didn't mean to do that." He gave her one of his big cocky grins and slid an arm around her shoulders. "But don't you worry none. Not when you've got big strong Chuckie here to protect you."

Yeah, but who'd protect her from *him?* She ducked away, pretending to inspect the new English saddle Cord had bought her last month. "I can take care of myself. I just don't like anyone sneaking up on me."

He laughed. "Now, darlin', I didn't do any sneaking. As a matter of fact, I do believe I was here first. Even thought you might have come out here to see me."

Bri gave him a bland look but then laughed at the wounded look on his face. Of course it was an act, but he had the hangdog expression down so well.

"You might as well make yourself useful. Help me count these snaffle bits."

"What for?"

"It's inventory time."

Chuck frowned. "No kiddin'. You guys keep track of that kind of stuff?"

"Of course. This is a business."

"Wow! Pretty and smart, too." He slid an arm around her waist and urged her toward him.

Bri gave him a none-too-gentle shove. He wasn't usually so touchy, even though she'd heard rumors about his womanizing from Jessica Grayson and Hannah Coleman. If he thought he could take liberties because Cord was away, he had another thing coming.

"I can handle the inventory," she said with a warning look. "Why don't you go back to doing whatever it was you were doing."

"Hell, I'm sorry, Brianna. I didn't mean nothin'." His blues eyes sparkling, he gave her that boyish grin again. It did make him look awfully cute. "Don't hold my friendly country ways against me."

Trying not to smile, she raised her eyebrows. "I heard you were from Dallas."

"True enough. But when my daddy left me and my mama, we moved up to the Panhandle to be near my grandparents. Ever been up there, darlin'?"

Bri's heart squeezed as she shook her head. She knew more than she cared to about being abandoned.

"Don't guess you would've had reason to visit that part of the state. Ain't nothin' there." He winked. "Especially since I've left."

She laughed. "You *are* something, that's for sure.

Now, would you leave me alone so I can finish my work?"

His expression got serious suddenly. "Are you going to be leavin' the Flying Ace anytime soon?"

"Why would you say that?" she asked, knowing full well the reason.

"Me and the boys were talkin' and..." He shrugged. "I guess now that the boss is married, we figured you might not want to stick around."

"This is my home, too." She turned away and picked up the clipboard so he couldn't see how much the idea of leaving frightened her.

"I know that, darlin', it's just, I dunno—"

"Don't call me darlin'." Her hands shook, but she tried to hold the pen steady as she made a notation about the condition of the work saddles.

"Now, no need to get all prickly. Of course, I'm hopin' you don't go. I imagine that house is plenty big enough for two women."

Bri focused on the clipboard, unsure how much her eyes would give away. "I can't imagine that you all don't have enough work to do that you have time to discuss my future."

"Whew!" Chuck removed his Stetson and wiped his forehead with the back of his sleeve. "It's gettin' mighty hot in here. I best wait till it cools down before I ask you what I came to ask."

She slanted him a sidelong glance. He was grinning like the Cheshire cat. Darn it. Now he'd stirred her curiosity.

"What?"

"I don't want to ask you when you're so steamed."

She sighed and lowered the clipboard. "I'm not mad. I just don't like people speculating on my personal business."

"It wasn't like that at all, darlin'. Honest." He hunched his shoulders. "Me and the boys just don't want to see you go. Me, especially."

Bri turned away again. Why hadn't she just let the subject drop? She didn't care what Chuck wanted to ask her anymore. She wanted him to leave. She just wanted to be alone. She faced him, ready to tell him to go.

He twirled his Stetson in his hands and for the first time she could recall, he looked unsure. "Next week is the Bridle dance and I was wonderin' if you'd like to go."

A dance? She nearly dropped the clipboard.

"With me, of course." He raked a hand through his sandy-colored hair. "I mean, the other guys are goin', too, but I want you to be my date."

Bri cleared her throat. "I don't think so."

"You already have a date?"

"No, I won't be going."

Chuck drew his head back in surprise. "Everyone's goin'. The dance is a big deal in Bridle."

"I don't like to dance," she murmured as she ran a finger down the list of inventory items.

"Why not?"

"You won't eat beets."

He blinked. "So?"

"Well, why not?"

Chuck scratched his head and then set his hat back

on. "Darlin', there ain't one blessed thing that dancin' and beets have in common. And that's a fact."

Bri sighed and shook her head. So he was cute. Just not the sharpest tool in the shed. "Thank you for asking. But I won't be going."

"Come on, Brianna. Don't say no yet. Think about it. The prettiest girl in the whole dang county can't sit out the dance. It ain't right."

She blushed and bowed her head. "Get out of here and let me get my work done, or I won't be going anywhere."

"So, you'll think about it?"

She still wouldn't look up, but she heard the grin in his voice. "Goodbye, Chuck."

"I'll take that as a maybe." He laughed. "See you later, darlin'."

She kept her gaze on the clipboard until she was sure he'd left the stables, and then she sagged against the pole, tempted to slide down and crawl into a ball in the hay. It wasn't bad enough that she had doubts about her place here at the Flying Ace, but others were talking about it, too.

Maybe she should go to the dance. Start circulating. Meet other ranchers. She'd learned enough about the business in the past year that she could get a job at another ranch. Bridle was a small, tight community, and the odds of a position being open were slim, but there were neighboring communities, and around here everything was done by word of mouth.

But a dance? The thought made her shudder.

Aunt Elaine hadn't believed in any situation that allowed a boy and girl to get that close, and had forbidden Bri from attending any of the high-school dances. She'd snuck out once, on the pretense of going to the library, but the evening had been a nightmare.

Her clothes had been all wrong. She'd been woefully ignorant of the latest dance steps. Not that she'd been all that familiar with the old ones. All she knew was that dancing was not her cup of tea.

The clipboard slipped from her fingers and fell into the hay. She bent to retrieve it and when she came back up, she saw Rafe standing near the rear door. Not looking as if he'd just arrived.

Her pulse picked up speed and her hand automatically went to her hair. Her ponytail was a mess. "What are you doing here?"

His gaze followed the path Chuck had taken out of the stables. "I thought you had work to do."

"I do. I—" She didn't answer to him. "I thought you were going to the Desert Rose."

"I'm taking one of the horses."

She hid a smile, unable to picture him driving the pickup she'd offered. Even in jeans, a chambray shirt and boots, he looked different from the other guys around Bridle. More sophisticated. Worldly. Exotic.

Definitely more attractive.

No one else gave her that funny flutter in her tummy.

"Is everything all right?" He narrowed his gaze and then again looked toward the door by which Chuck had left.

"Fine." She wondered how much he'd heard. "Why wouldn't it be?"

"A woman such as yourself has many admirers. Sometimes their attention can seem overwhelming."

"Admirers?" Her cheeks burned and she hugged the clipboard to her chest. "Don't be silly."

He frowned slightly. "You must not take these young men's intentions lightly."

Intentions? She wasn't going to ask. "Help yourself to any of the horses. Cord favors Lightning, the tan gelding, when his horse is being groomed."

Rafe stared at her, his dark eyes intense and probing, making her want to confess to sins she hadn't even committed.

"I have to get back to work," she said, and turned away from him. Nothing on the paper attached to the clipboard made sense anymore, but it gave her something to focus on.

"Brianna?"

"I'll have something made for lunch around one. If I'm not around, check the refrigerator."

He touched her arm and she stiffened. "Why are you so uneasy around me?"

"I'm not." Heat climbed her neck, and when he urged her to turn around, she lowered her lashes.

"What am I to think but that Aliah has said unkind things about me?"

"That's not true." Her gaze flew to his face and she saw the amusement he couldn't quite hide. "Okay, so *you* make me a little nervous. I don't know why. Probably because I'd never met a sheikh before."

"Now that you have, am I so different than any other man?"

"I guess not," she said, lying through her teeth. He was different, all right. Taller, darker, more self-assured than any of the guys she knew. And when he smiled. Lord help her. Maybe it was a good thing he didn't smile all that often.

"Tell me, who was that young man with whom you were speaking?"

"Chuck Williams. He works here." She narrowed her gaze. "Why?"

"In your brother's absence, I hope you feel free to come to me if you have any problems."

She stared at him in disbelief. "I thought you said Cord was only teasing about asking you to watch over me?"

"I am an older brother. I would want someone to take care of Aliah in my absence. In effect, now that she has married, I have handed her over to Cord. It is not unusual for a brother to—"

She made a most unladylike sound of frustration, and then clamped her mouth shut when she realized what she'd done.

His eyebrows drew together in a slight frown. "You are upset."

"Not really." Embarrassed was more like it. Aunt Elaine would be mortified and furious at Bri's manners. Of course, since leaving New Hampshire, Bri had changed in a lot of ways. Thanks to Cord, she had more freedom than she'd ever dreamed possible. "It's just that—" She shook her head. "It's not important. I apologize for overreacting."

He stared at her, his dark eyes searching, and for a moment she feared he wouldn't let the matter drop.

Not that she had any intention of discussing the importance of her newfound independence. Such as it was. Here at the Flying Ace the crippling shyness that had stunted her social life seemed to ease. She felt safe here. At peace. But if she had to venture out into the world again...

She couldn't even finish the thought.

"No need for an apology, I assure you."

"You're right." At his surprised look, she swallowed. "I'm your hostess while my brother is away, not your ward." There. She'd said it. "Not that I don't appreciate your concern." She sighed at the unnecessary concession.

Rafe's left eyebrow went up, and she couldn't tell if he was annoyed or amused.

She didn't care. She'd said her piece and she wasn't sorry. "Now, if you will excuse me..."

He touched her arm when she started to turn away. "Answer one question first."

"Okay," she said slowly. "If I can."

"Why would you not want to go to this dance in town?"

She lifted her chin. "You were listening?"

"I overheard. There is a difference."

Amusement and not annoyance had been on his face, she decided. The look was still there. Condescending, almost paternal. She had a good mind to wrap her arms around his neck and kiss him so hard he'd never think of her as a child again.

The mere idea stole her breath. She could no more do something like that than ride bareback in a rodeo. Heck, she still had trouble staying in a saddle. Lots of dogs and cats roamed her New Hampshire neighborhood. No horses.

Texas was a whole new world to her.

So was Rafe.

She swallowed hard at the way he stared into her eyes as if he could read her every thought. "I really have to get back to work."

"Then I will assist you."

That startled a laugh out of her. "You? Work?"

Anger flared briefly in his eyes. "The idea surprises you?"

"Well, you couldn't even get your own breakfast." She bit her lip, wishing she hadn't said that.

"Ah, how do you know that was not a ploy to assure myself of your company?"

She blinked. "Huh?"

He laughed, and his whole face changed. "Perhaps I am not the man of leisure you assume."

"I didn't assume any such thing. Allie told me how much you do for Munir."

"Ah, but you think I am ignorant of the mundane tasks of life."

"Well…" Bri thought about Allie's first attempts at manual labor and she had to stifle a laugh. "Actually, yes, I do."

His features tightened. "Your honesty is admirable."

"Not that I'm being critical. There's been no need for you or Allie to do things for yourselves."

"While I was at the university, you would be surprised at what I learned to do for myself." One side of his mouth lifted and made her wonder what exactly he meant. "Allie did not go away to school and as a result became very pampered."

"But she's not anymore. She does a lot around here to help. Heck, before long Cord won't need—" She gasped, horrified at what she was about to say.

Quickly, she turned back to sorting the bits. She'd already lost count of the bridles. After an hour she'd accomplished nothing. If she couldn't be useful in the business end of the ranch, no one would need her.

When Rafe remained silent for too long, she finally slid him a glance. And wished she hadn't. The sympathy she saw in his eyes made her ill.

"Brianna." He took her hand and she was too stunned to pull away. "Just because a man takes a wife does not mean he does not need his sister."

"You don't understand." She looked down at the toes of her tennis shoes, trying to gather her thoughts, willing herself not to say anything foolish.

He stroked the inside of her wrist with his thumb, and her breath caught. "I understand that you mean a great deal to Cord."

She met his eyes, and pulled her hand away. "You don't know him. You can't say that."

"Ah, but I am only repeating something he told me."

"I don't believe you."

He smiled. "He also said you were shy, but he neglected to mention refreshingly honest."

This conversation was not helping. In fact, hurt seeped into the fear. Just how intimately had Cord discussed her with Rafe?

As if reading her mind, Rafe sobered. "Your

brother spoke of you only in terms of a warning to me.''

"A warning?"

"I told him how extraordinarily beautiful you are and he told me to…'' His dark brows drew together in a puzzled frown. "The saying escapes me. Ah, I believe the term he used was 'hands off.'''

Bri's mouth opened but nothing came out. Rafe thought *she* was beautiful. How was that possible? And then she blinked. "Cord said what?''

"Do not look so troubled. He is your brother, your patron. As we discussed earlier, of course he would defend you.''

Bri shook her head. No sense trying to get through either of their thick, chauvinistic skulls. And then she drew in her lower lip, wondering what Rafe's response had been. Not that she'd ask him. Not in a million years.

"I have an idea.'' He took her hand again.

She gave him a cautious look.

"Go to the Desert Rose with me.''

The heat from his palm pressed to hers traveled up her arm and went straight to her belly. "Why?''

"To watch Mac Coleman train the two new colts. I believe one of them is Rising Star.''

No fair. He knew she had a special fondness for the scrawny colt. Although the way Rafe rubbed the inside of her wrist again was an even more persuasive argument. "You forget I have work to do.''

"It will still be here.''

She hesitated, afraid to meet his eyes.

"Hey, Bri. I almost forgot to ask—''

At the sound of Chuck's voice, she gave a guilty start and tried to jerk her hand away. Rafe held firm.

Chuck stared at them, obviously startled himself, and then his gaze fell to their clasped hands and his lips thinned.

"Sorry," he muttered in a sarcastic voice. "Didn't mean to crash the party."

With a firm tug, Bri withdrew her hand. She was embarrassed. No getting around it, but she'd be damned if she'd let Chuck get away with acting like a two-year-old and give her that accusatory glare. "You wanted something?" Amazingly her voice didn't crack.

He glowered at Rafe and then gave her a wounded look. "Never mind."

"Chuck, come on. You didn't interrupt, and you obviously wanted something."

"It's personal," Chuck said, darting Rafe a sour glance. "I'll talk to you later."

Rafe didn't offer to leave but stood there, looking bored and impatient, which really annoyed her. In fact, both men annoyed her.

"Fine, then if you'll both get out of my hair, I can finish this inventory."

Rafe frowned, his displeasure clear. "I thought we had a date."

Her gaze immediately went to Chuck, whose eyes had narrowed in contempt. "To watch Mac train over at the Desert Rose? I'd hardly call that a date."

"Afterward, I will take you to lunch," he said as if the matter was settled, and then reached for her hand again.

She had just enough wits about her to jerk away, but words failed her. What the heck was he doing? The whole bunkhouse would be gossiping about them by dinnertime. She couldn't bear the thought. Enough of her life had been hurt by rumors and whispers. All that talk about how she was unwanted, a bastard child…

"Okay, I get the picture." Chuck took a step back, his expression far from understanding. "But you could've told me, Bri, and not waste my time."

She threw up her hands. "Told you what?"

"That you two were already playing footsies under the table." Lifting his chin in a cocky manner, he adjusted his Stetson.

"We are not." She looked to Rafe for help. Maybe he didn't understand what Chuck was getting at, because he just stood there watching with lazy interest.

"Yeah, well, that's sure what it seemed like." Chuck slid Rafe an accusing look, which was received with a stifled yawn.

"Well, I'm telling you how it is." Bri put her hands on her hips. "Not that I owe you an explanation."

"Sure enough, darlin'," Chuck shrugged and took a step back. "Just wish you hadn't led me on about the dance."

"I never—" She could end the talk before it started. "Who said I led you on? Of course I'll go to the dance with you."

Chapter Four

"I didn't know you were still here." Mac Coleman passed the reins of the colt with whom he'd been working to one of the hands, and headed toward the risers where Rafe sat and watched with keen interest for the past hour.

The Arabians the Desert Rose turned out were superb in both breeding and temperament. He had found none comparable in the Mideast or Texas. "I have business in Dallas at the week's end. However, I will stay until the foal I have purchased is born."

"Hannah, Alex's wife who is also a vet, tells me that'll be any day now." Mac took off his hat, wiped his face with a kerchief and then reached for a bottle of water he had left near the stairs to the bleachers.

He uncapped it, took a big gulp, and then added, "I hope Anastasia gives birth before you leave. That mare is as stubborn as they come."

"If not, I have no choice but to go to Dallas. However, I will return the next day."

Mac's eyebrows rose. "Just for the birth?"

Rafe gave a slight shrug. "I would like to see my sister again before I return to Munir."

Mac smiled. "I take it you're not still mad at her."

"Furious."

Mac laughed. "Yeah. But Cord's a good guy."

Rafe nodded. That was his only comfort. The knowledge that Aliah was happy and would be well cared for would ease the harsh criticism awaiting him.

"Where are you staying?" Mac shaded his eyes and focused on something in the direction of the stables.

"At the Flying Ace."

"Makes sense." He glanced toward the stables again. "Mickey is bringing Rising Star. Are you going to stick around?"

"If you do not mind an audience."

"Of course not. Afterward we'll go back to the house and have a beer." Mac headed toward the colt, calling out instructions to the hired hand as he went.

Rafe smiled. Americans certainly loved their beer. Not even while attending Harvard had he acquired a taste for the brew. He had always preferred wine, much to the amusement of his fellow classmates who had begun facetiously calling him "Your Highness."

In those days he had been hot-tempered and arrogant. No one in Munir would have dared to treat him in such a manner. He was treated with respect and people scurried to do his bidding. Not so at Harvard.

His education at the American university had gone far beyond academics. He had learned tolerance and humility and the art of negotiation. Especially since no one at Harvard was particularly anxious to respond to his demands. He smiled at the memories. Good friends had eventually been made, and there he had become a man.

"Mind if I sit with you?"

The feminine voice startled him. A redheaded woman in tight faded jeans had started up the steps. The Colemans' daughter, he was fairly certain. But he could not remember her name.

"Please." He stood.

"Sit," she said and settled in beside him. "I don't know if you recall, but we met briefly at Allie's wedding. "I'm Jessica Coleman. I mean, Grayson." Pink tinted her cheeks and a beautiful smile lifted her lips. "I got married recently."

"Must be contagious."

She grinned. "Then you'd better be careful."

He smiled back. She was a delightful young lady... though mischievous, like Aliah.

Brianna was different.

Why she had suddenly come to mind, he could not fathom. In fact, the thought startled him.

"He's a beauty, isn't he?"

Rafe followed her gaze out to the arena. Mac led Rising Star around in a circle. The colt's coat shimmered in the Texas sun like fine brown silk. "You have the finest Arabians I have ever seen. Your family has established quite a venerable reputation."

Jessica nodded, her gaze fastened to the man and horse. "They take a lot of pride in their work. But besides that, they all love horses. So do I, but I'm on the business end of things." She turned to him with a puzzled frown. "You aren't staying at the Desert Rose, are you?'

"No, the Flying Ace."

"Haven't Cord and Allie left?"

He nodded. "The day before yesterday."

"But..." She blinked. "You're staying with Brianna?"

He nodded again, and turned his attention toward Rising Star.

"Does Cord know?"

Rafe smiled and glanced her way. "Of course."

She flushed. "Of course," she repeated, and refocused her gaze on the training.

"Is there anything wrong?" he asked, amused at her flustered demeanor.

"Nothing." She straightened and brought up a hand to shade her eyes. "Speaking of nothing..."

He turned around to see what had caught her attention. Brianna approached from the direction of the house. Even though she was still a distance away, there was no mistaking her blond hair or the long, lean legs bringing her closer to him. His heart took an unexpected leap.

"Gee, I wonder what's brought her out here in the middle of the afternoon?" Jessica's voice, iced with meaning, doused him like a cold shower.

He did not care for the insinuation in her tone. "I have no inkling. I asked her to accompany me, but she had work to do."

"Hmm, apparently her priorities have changed." Jessica did not even give him a glance, but there was no mistaking the amusement in her voice.

His annoyance soared. He understood the possible appearance of impropriety of him staying alone at the house, with Brianna being a single woman, but Americans were usually more open-minded about such things. Besides, Brianna was just a child.

As she got closer, the light breeze molded her blouse to her breasts and something stirred deep in his belly. Feeling the weight of her stare, he looked at Jessica. Her rapt attention was focused on him, the speculation in her eyes most disquieting.

Slowly she dragged her gaze away. "Hey, Bri."

"Hello, Jessie." Brianna stopped at the foot of the risers and squinted up at them. Even with the sun directly in her face, her pale skin was flawless. "I didn't know you were still in town. I thought you went back to Dallas. Is Nick with you?"

Jessica sighed. "No, he had Coleman-Grayson business in Houston and I have some here. I'll see him this weekend. Maybe we could get together..." Jessica cast a curious glance at Rafe. "If you have time."

Brianna, on the other hand, carefully avoided his eyes. "Of course I do. You name the time and I'll be ready."

And then she finally looked at him and blushed. He directed his attention to the arena. No sense in pointing out she had adamantly claimed to have no time for him. He still did not understand why she had gotten so angry at the stables. Perhaps that Chuck fellow meant more to her than she had admitted.

The possibility chafed. Even though Rafe knew it had nothing to with him.

His jaw clenched as she climbed the risers to join them, her hair, uncharacteristically out of her pony-tail, was caught by the breeze and fanned out like a silken sail. Her worn jeans hugged her hips and thighs, showing off her lean curves.

The hell her relationship with the hired hand had nothing to with Rafe! he thought. He wanted her. He had from the first moment he saw her. He could deny it to others but not to himself. In effect, he had denied it during the past few days. Heavily denied it when Cord had asked him to look out for her. But he could no longer ignore the attraction.

She was perfection. Her hair, her face, the clear blue of her eyes, the shy way she looked at him. He liked her cool reserve that reminded him of the blond American actress who had married the prince of Monaco.

Yet despite her timidity, Brianna was intelligent and business-minded, with enough fire to tempt him. Perhaps even challenge him.

Upon returning to Munir after Harvard, he was often chided for having developed a taste for American women. He had dismissed the taunts. But they were true. *That* he had known all along. And, Brianna, Aliah's new sister-in-law, the woman he had vowed to watch over, embodied his ultimate fantasy.

Damn, he had obviously gone too long without a woman.

Perhaps in Dallas he could remedy the situation. His gaze drew back to Brianna. Maybe he should go to Dallas early. Possibly tonight.

"Check out Rising Star," Jessica told her with a

nudge of her chin toward the arena. "He's a beauty, all right. No wonder Mac has a soft touch for that one."

"Is he already sold?" Brianna settled down next to Jessica, away from Rafe.

"I don't think so. Why? You interested?"

Brianna blinked at her friend. "Me?" And then her longing gaze went back to Rising Star. "What would I do with such a fine horse?"

"Uh, ride him?"

Brianna slid her a wry look. And then her eyes met Rafe's. She quickly glanced away. "Rising Star is a show horse. Everyone should be allowed to see him."

Rafe smiled to himself, watching the way her worshipful gaze followed the colt. "I agree. An animal of such beauty should be shared. However, someone who appreciates his value must be his patron."

Brianna and Jessica both gave him odd looks.

"So, anyway, what brings you by?" Jessica asked her friend.

Brianna put a hand to her mouth. "Oh my God." Her gaze flew to Rafe. "You had a phone call."

"From Dallas?"

"Munir."

Frowning, he checked his cell phone. It was on. No messages. "They said it was urgent?"

Brianna's face colored and her gaze skittered toward Jessica. "I assumed it was."

Jessica grinned. "How nice of you to come all this way to get him."

Brianna's color deepened and she got to her feet. "I'd better get back to work."

Rafe stood, as well. "I will go with you."

"You can't. I mean, I brought Cord's truck."

He knew he did not have to hurry back. If the call had been urgent, they would have tried his cell phone first. But he was also pleased that Brianna had come for him. "Perhaps I can ride back with you and get my horse later."

"Sure," Jessica interjected. "I'll make sure he's taken to the stable and fed."

Brianna stuffed her hands into the pockets of her jeans and shrugged. "Going on horseback is just as fast."

"True." Rafe bowed slightly. "But then I would not have the pleasure of your company,"

Her lips parted in surprise. The color had begun to fade from her face but blossomed once more. She cast a helpless glance at Jessica.

The other woman laughed with glee. "Go ahead, Rafe. I'll arrange to have someone take care of your horse."

"Thank you. Please tell Mac I will see him later."

"This doesn't make sense," Brianna murmured as she took the lead down the risers.

Most pleased to follow, Rafe's gaze stayed on the tempting swell of her backside. It had taken him a while to become accustomed to women wearing pants, but when he realized the advantage jeans provided, he had quickly grown to like the attire.

"Bye, you two." Jessica waved, grinning, making it a point that they had left without saying goodbye.

They stepped off the risers and exchanged a glance. With a sheepish wince, Brianna quickly looked away.

"I'll call you later, Jessie," she said. "Maybe we could go to dinner in town one night."

"Sure. If you aren't too busy."

Brianna gave her friend a meaningful look, and then hurried toward the house. In a couple of strides, Rafe was beside her.

"How very kind of you to interrupt your work to come and get me."

"Think nothing of it."

"What an odd saying. I do not believe I have heard it before."

She gave him a suspicious glance. "It means, no problem, that the gesture meant nothing."

"Ah, but it does. You were so angry with me earlier. You could have let the call wait until I returned."

She sighed. "I was never angry with you."

"Earlier, when I so rudely interfered with you and your young man. I do hope—"

She stopped and faced him, her eyes sparkling with temper. "He is not my young man. I don't even want to go to the dance with him."

"But you accepted."

"What else was I supposed to do? He thought there was something going on between—" She bit her lip, and then resumed her pace. "Never mind."

"Brianna." He touched her arm and she stiffened. "Explain the problem to me."

When she refused to answer, he saw the pickup parked in the driveway and decided to wait. There would be enough time to talk on the drive back, where he would have her undistracted attention.

Once they were on their way to the Flying Ace,

Rafe remained quiet. In his experience, women were uncomfortable with silence. He would wait, let her speak first, let her explain.

But as he had already guessed, Brianna was not like most women.

They turned onto the gravel driveway where the white wooden sign announced the Flying Ace, and still she had said nothing nor spared him a glance. His only consolation was the unfettered time it gave him to study her profile.

Not until the house became visible through a thicket of trees did she look his way. "What?"

He frowned.

"Why are you staring at me?"

The tires hit a rut in the road, causing the truck to bounce to the left, and she quickly returned her attention to driving.

"You are very beautiful. I would think you are accustomed to having men stare at you."

Her gaze snapped his way and they hit another rut. "Are you teasing me?"

"Teasing?" He reared his head back. She looked serious. "Of course not. I was merely stating a fact."

Her grip visibly tightened on the wheel and she slowed the truck. Her mouth opened, but nothing came out.

"Have I embarrassed you?"

"No." She nodded. "Yes."

"I apologize. It certainly was not my intention." He studied her for a moment longer, all the more intrigued by her modesty.

"Let's forget it," she said, darting him a shy look

before steering the truck toward the garage on the right.

"Tell me something before we park, this lake that is nearby. Can we get there by car?"

Reluctance showed in the clenching of her jaw, the way she gripped the wheel. "No."

"By horse?"

She nodded.

"Is it within walking distance?"

"Probably." She moistened her lips, the pink tip of her tongue momentarily distracting him. "But it would be quite a hike. I doubt you'd want to do that."

"You seem reluctant to tell me about this place. Is it private?"

"Of course not." She brought the truck to a stop. "Cord owns the land on one side of the water, and the Colemans own the other side."

"Good. I will take a ride later and look for myself."

She pulled the keys from the ignition and tucked them into her pocket. "You'll probably be disappointed, but suit yourself."

She got out of the truck before he could go around and open her door. American women tended to shun the tradition, which sometimes annoyed him. The gesture was merely a courtesy, and had nothing to do with usurping their independence.

He joined her as she left the garage and headed for the house. She did not break her stride in her haste to get inside.

Or away from him.

The notion was most irritating. That a woman

would not want his attention was as foreign to him as the strange dish of prairie oysters.

"Hey, Bri, wait up."

At the sound of the male voice coming from behind them, she stopped and turned. Rafe did, as well. One of the ranch hands approached. He had obviously been out on the range. Dust flew from his hat when he removed it, and his jeans and chaps were grimy with dirt and sweat.

Brianna gave him a big smile. "Hey, Manny, what's up?" The man grunted. "Taxes and my blood pressure."

She laughed. "I'm afraid I can't do anything about either of those problems."

"Well, ma'am, you can help my blood pressure some." He nodded acknowledgment to Rafe. "I need a purchase order for more barbed wire. That scatter-brained Chuck didn't pick up near enough for mending the south pasture fences."

"No problem. If you want, I'll call the order in. How much do you need?"

Rafe watched as she helped the older man calculate the amount of fencing required. That he was a mess and smelled rather pungent did not seem to offend her. She was patient when he had trouble adding figures, and waited for him to gather his thoughts. She kept the information in her head, and promised to call the order in immediately.

"Thanks, Bri. As soon as they have the stuff ready, I'll pull a man off branding to pick it up." He put his hat back on. "You just let me know."

"Tell you what," she said. "I'll put a rush on the

order and then pick it up myself. You just make sure there's someone to unload it when I get back."

Rafe stiffened. She sure had a lot of time for everyone but him.

"You're a doll, Bri." The man had started to back away, but then he frowned and stopped. "Chuck's going around telling everybody you're going to the dance with him. Tell me it ain't so. You ain't going with that numbskull, are you?"

Brianna blushed. "So what if I am?"

Manny shook his head. "Besides the fact that you're too good for that sneaky sidewinder, Cord wouldn't like it. Not one bit."

Her chin lifted and she placed her hands on her hips. "Would you kindly explain to me how this is your concern?"

The man frowned. "Don't go getting your back up. You know how much me and the boys like you. We don't want to see you hooking up with the likes of him. The guy's a damn skirt chaser. Ask anybody."

Her expression softened. "I appreciate your concern. I do." She slid Rafe an uneasy glance. "But you don't have to worry about me falling for Chuck. It's just a dance. That's all."

"Then I suppose me and the boys better explain that to him so he don't go getting any ideas."

Brianna sighed. "You will not. I'm an adult, Manny. I can take care of myself."

Rafe laughed quietly, and they both looked at him. Cord need not have worried. The men all wanted to protect her from the young stud. He gave a slight bow. "My apology. My thoughts were elsewhere."

The older man hunched his shoulders. "Sorry," he mumbled, his gaze lingering on Rafe. "Didn't mean to bring up personal business in front of him."

Brianna sighed again.

"Do not concern yourself." Rafe took her by the elbow. "I am now family. I, too, will go to the dance. As Brianna's chaperon."

Chapter Five

The rest of the day Brianna alternated from furious to hopelessly excited. Rafe had no right to insinuate himself as her chaperon. No right at all. Yet the idea of him going to the dance with her...well, not with her...but sort of...

She grunted with disgust. She had no business having these thoughts. None. Almost twenty-three and he thought she needed a chaperon? Well, he had another think coming.

Dismayed, she stared into her closet. Jeans, jeans and more jeans. The three dresses she did own looked as if they belonged to a schoolgirl. Good grief, had she really worn those? Of course, Aunt Elaine had selected them, so it was no wonder they were so dowdy. The truth was, if she were just going with Chuck she wouldn't care about wearing the schoolgirl dresses. But now that Rafe would be there...

Darn it! That shouldn't matter. Not one tiny bit.

But it did. It mattered a lot. Too much.

She wrapped her arms around herself, fell back on the bed and stared at the ceiling. She hadn't been able to think straight for a week. If she finished her inventory by fiscal year-end it would be a darn miracle.

Rafe was getting under her skin. Even before he'd come to get Allie, Bri had been enthralled with him. Not just because of the stories Allie had told, but she'd shown Bri a picture of him from five years ago at Allie's "coming-out" ball.

Tall, dark and handsome in his formal clothes, he'd stolen Bri's breath away. He'd looked like a prince out of a fairy tale, his eyes so dark and intense they made her shiver. She'd had a dozen fantasies about him, racy fantasies of which she hadn't known she was capable, and then he'd shown up at their doorstep.

Well, he wouldn't be here much longer. Too bad the thought didn't cheer her.

The truth was, she liked that he made her heart race, her palms clammy, and her tummy flutter. The feelings were scary and nice and very different from anything else she'd experienced. Sure, she'd thought Rich Simpson had been pretty hot stuff in the tenth grade. She'd actually prayed, on her knees, every night for a week that he'd ask her to the winter ball. But he'd asked Sally Monroe instead. Luckily, it had only taken Bri two days to get over him.

And then in senior year she'd had a mad crush on Tony McMann. He'd made her pulse go haywire, too, and he had asked her out. But the jerk had been all hands and no couth and pretty much made her decide she'd had it with men for a while. College had been all about studying and winning top grades so that she could find a great job and get out from under Aunt Elaine's thumb.

Not that she hadn't been grateful to her aunt. At least she hadn't thrown Bri out after her mother had dumped her in Elaine's lap before running off to get into more trouble. It couldn't have been easy for the older woman, a spinster by choice, to raise someone else's child. Yes, she'd complained, bitterly at times, but she'd always seen to it that Bri was fed and clothed and educated, and for that, Bri would always be grateful.

How wonderful her life was now. Free. Peaceful. Exciting and romantic, too. So vastly different from the quiet New England village she'd known all her life. She looked out her window toward the north pasture where emerald green rolling slopes met the clear blue sky.

God, she prayed she didn't have to leave.

She sat upright. She couldn't think about that right now. No use borrowing trouble, as her aunt had told her a million times. Besides, Bri had a more immediate problem. Like what to wear to the darn dance next week.

Another unsettling thought pricked her, and she half laughed, half moaned. Heck, she didn't even know how to dance.

"I'M NOT SURE." Brianna pinched the silky dress between her thumb and forefinger. The fabric felt heavenly, but the color...

"Why don't you try it on?" Peggy Sue took the dress from Bri's hands and held it up to her. "I think it's fabulous. And not because I want to make the sale. This dress is you, honey. Give me a bible and I'll swear on it."

"I don't know." Bri worried her lower lip. "I've never worn red before."

"Go on. Try it." The short plump saleswoman gave her a gentle shove toward the fitting room. "You'll see I'm right."

Brianna had nearly not come into the store when she saw that Peggy Sue was working the afternoon shift. She liked the older woman well enough, but she was pushy and loved to gossip. In fact, Bri was surprised the woman hadn't already asked about Rafe and why he was staying at the Flying Ace. She always seemed to know everything that went on around Bridle.

Because it was easier to try on the dress than argue with Peggy Sue, Bri draped it over her arm and then glanced over her shoulder to make sure Rafe hadn't sneaked into the store. He had a habit of popping up when least expected. Like when she'd been ready to come into town to pick up the barbed wire. She'd barely gotten the truck door open when he appeared and announced he'd be going along for the ride.

"How about this one?" Peggy Sue studied the lines of a royal-blue shift that looked entirely too short. "It's a little plain but I think it would be stunning on you."

Bri promptly added the dress to the red one. "I'd better try these on now. I don't have much time."

She sent another nervous glance over her shoulder. The barbed wire should be loaded by now. Rafe had agreed to wait for the men to finish while she ran an errand.

"Who came with you?" Peggy Sue went to the window and craned her neck to see down the sidewalk. "That pretty new wife of Cord's?"

"No, they're on their honeymoon. Is this hand-washable?" Bri asked to distract the woman.

Frowning, Peggy Sue waddled toward Bri and lifted the reading glasses she wore on a pink ribbon around her neck onto her nose. She took the dress out of Bri's hands and peered at the label. "Well, it says so right here, doesn't it?"

"Oh, yeah, I guess so."

The woman stared at Bri over her glasses. "Child, you're as nervous as a long-tailed cat in a roomful of rockers. What's the matter?"

"Nothing." She forced a smile. "I'd better go try these on."

"Come on, honey, you can tell Peggy Sue."

"It's nothing. Really."

"Is it about the dance?" The woman's features softened. "Surely a pretty thing like you won't be going alone."

"I'm going with someone." Bri backed toward the dressing room, trying to shoot a furtive look out the window.

"Oh." Peggy Sue's voice rose with curiosity. "Who?"

"Just one of the hands. I doubt you know him. He's kind of new around here."

The clerk's expression darkened. "Not that Chuck idiot. That no-good skunk took Molly Holmes out twice, sweet-talked her into going to San Antonio with him for the weekend, and then dropped her like a hot potato.''

Bri groaned and slipped behind the curtain. She should have known Peggy Sue knew Chuck. The woman made it her business to know everyone within a hundred-mile radius. "I do have this one small problem, Peggy Sue," Bri said, knowing if she threw out a bone, the woman would forget about Chuck.

"Oh, what's that?"

Bri let her wait while she pulled off her shirt. "It's kind of personal."

"Well, you know me. I won't tell a soul." Her voice had gotten closer, directly on the other side of the curtain.

Holding back a laugh, Bri slid her jeans off and hung them on the hook on the back wall. "It's really kind of silly."

"If you're fretting over it, then it's best to talk about the problem."

Mean to lead her on, Bri knew, but all she wanted to do was try on the dresses and get out of here. "It's about the dance."

"Yes?"

She slipped the red dress on first and stood back to look in the small mirror. The fitting room was so small it was hard to get an accurate picture, but no way was she going beyond that curtain. Of course, Peggy Sue was sufficiently distracted.

"Brianna?"

"Yes."

"For goodness' sakes, child, I thought you died

and went to heaven already. Are you going to spit it out?''

"Oh, I just tried on the red dress."

"Well, step on out here and show me."

"It didn't fit," she said as she studied the way the fabric hugged her breasts, not bothered by the small fib she'd just told. The dress wouldn't do, the neckline was too low, and she didn't need Peggy Sue trying to tell her otherwise. "I'll try the blue one."

"Fine. Now, you tell Peggy Sue what's bothering you, honey."

"Okay, but it's really silly."

"Doggone it. You're making me wait on purpose, aren't you?"

Bri grinned at herself in the mirror before she yanked the red dress over her head. "Why, Peggy Sue, I would never do that. I know how much you're trying to help, and all."

"Of course I am."

"I know." She glanced at the blue dress, decided against trying it on and grabbed her jeans. "It's about the dance."

"Yes?" The woman edged so close that Bri could see her outline in the curtain.

"I can't dance."

Peggy Sue hesitated. "And?"

"I'll have to sit in a corner and watch."

Bri let the silence stretch as she got into her clothes. Let Peggy Sue sulk for a minute. No doubt she felt cheated out of something juicier, but truthfully, the idea of even trying to dance did upset Bri.

"May I help you?"

Bri fastened her blouse buttons and frowned at the odd tone of Peggy Sue's voice. "No, thanks. I'm done trying these dresses on." She pushed back the curtain. "Maybe tomorrow—"

The words died on her tongue. Rafe stood near a rounder of dresses, fingering the silky fabric of a black dress Bri had considered trying on, and ignoring the way Peggy Sue gawked at him.

"No, thank you." He smiled at the woman. "I believe I have found what I was looking for." He raised his gaze to meet Brianna's eyes.

Her mouth still open, Peggy Sue slowly turned around to stare at Bri. "Is he yours?"

Heat filled Bri's cheeks. "Peggy Sue."

"I mean…" With narrowed eyes she looked from Bri to Rafe. "Is he with you?"

"Yes," Rafe said, his accent slightly more pronounced. "I am with Brianna. I am Ashraf Bahram, Rafe if you prefer." He gave her a bow of his head. "And you, charming lady, who might you be?"

Her eyes got wider than two half-dollars. "Are you one of them sheikhs who come to buy Arabians from the Desert Rose?"

"Yes."

Her hand went to her frizzy graying hair. "I'm Peggy Sue Miller. I'm half owner of this here store."

Bri tried not to roll her eyes. Everyone knew it was her daughter-in-law who owned the dress shop.

Rafe took Peggy Sue's hand and kissed the back of it. "I am most pleased to meet you."

She didn't pull her hand back for the longest time,

and when she finally did, she clutched it to her breasts and sighed.

The entire scene was quite pitiful. But it was a distraction, and for that Bri was grateful. She carried the two dresses back to the rounders and hung them. "I take it the barbed wire is all loaded up?"

"Yes, and I have brought the truck around to the front of the store."

"How did you know I was here?"

He smiled. "This is a small town, Brianna."

When his lips curved like that, and his gaze focused so intensely on her, as if she were the only woman on earth, she had no defenses. None. But he was right, and she'd best not forget that this was a small town and not much went unnoticed. She glanced over at Peggy Sue. The poor woman had probably never been speechless a day in her life before now.

It was kind of nice. Bri bit her lip at the uncharitable thought. "I'll come by later in the week, maybe Friday. Tell Rowena I said hi and give that cute little granddaughter of yours a hug for me."

Peggy Sue nodded, her gaze still fastened on Rafe. She gave him a faint smile and lifted her hand in farewell when Bri led him to the door.

Once they got outside, Bri went straight to the truck and got into the driver's side. Rafe took his time, stopping at the rear of the truck to test the security of the rolled bundles of wire.

She used the rearview mirror to watch him. No wonder Peggy Sue had gotten so tongue-tied. Bri had never really understood the term "cut a dashing figure'' until now. That's exactly what Rafe did. Especially in this fairly small Texas town.

Sure, he wore jeans like everyone else, except his were obviously a designer brand, but that wasn't even it. He was so tall and trim, so perfectly shaped that he could wear a feedbag and make it look good. His blue silk shirt was obviously tailor-made to resemble chambray, and fit his broad shoulders to perfection. On any other man in Bridle, silk would look horrid. In fact, no one would even dare to wear such a thing. The other guys would tease him mercilessly.

And the way he moved, with such casual elegance, almost as if he were playing a role on a stage, except he wasn't. That was just Rafe. His impeccable manners, his confidence, his sophistication were all as effortless and natural as breathing.

He clearly embodied royalty and good breeding, and although arrogance and ego lurked, he had the decency to keep them in check. And the common sense to make sure the barbed wire was secure.

She smiled at the thought. When she glanced into the rearview mirror again, he was gone. She twisted around in time to see him walk to the shop's door. Peggy Sue was standing at the threshold. Rafe said something and she nodded eagerly. What the heck was that about?

Bri turned back around, stared straight ahead and drummed her fingers on the wheel, tempted to leave him behind. What could he possibly have to say to Peggy Sue? Not that Bri would ask him. She wasn't that nosy. Of course she could call Peggy Sue once they got home.

He opened the passenger door, startling her.

She started the engine and revved it before he climbed in. All that got her were two annoyed looks from a couple getting out of their Chevy in front of Floyd's barbershop.

"Are you in a hurry to get home?" Rafe asked, looking totally unconcerned.

"The men are waiting for the wire."

"Surely we have time to stop for lunch."

Bri glanced at the dashboard clock. It was close to three. She'd totally forgotten to offer him anything. Of course, he knew where the kitchen was, darn it. "I can make a salad when we get home."

Not what he had in mind, judging from his sudden frown. "Are there no restaurants in town?"

"Well, yes, but—"

"How about there?" He gestured to the diner. Bridle's hotbed of gossip.

"I'm not sure you'd like the food," she said, driving past the diner.

"Why not?"

"It's just simple country food."

"I would like to try it."

"But the men need the wire."

He reached into his pocket and withdrew his cell phone. "Call them. An hour may not make a difference if they have embarked on other tasks."

"I can't call. They're out on the range."

He smiled. "I believe your foreman carries a phone of his own."

She sighed, and took the cell phone from him. His fingers brushed her hand, and it was darn pitiful the way her entire body reacted giddily to the casual touch. She pulled the truck to the curb before she punched in the number. The exercise was mostly for show. She already knew they didn't need the wire before morning.

"Okay," she said after she hung up and glanced in the side mirror to make a U-turn. "But if you don't like the food, don't blame me."

Rafe laughed, and even the way he did that was sexy and exotic and made her blush. How she would get through an entire meal with him while being the object of curious stares she had no idea. Maybe since it was such an odd time for lunch, she'd get lucky and the diner would be empty.

It wasn't too bad. Only two booths and one chair at the counter were occupied. Everyone turned around, though, as soon as they walked in, and all conversation came to a dead stop.

"Hi, Rosie." Bri waved to the owner.

The redhead had been leaning on the counter talking to Pearl Applebee from the fabric shop next door, but she promptly put out her cigarette and grabbed a couple of menus. She was a good-natured woman who laughed at all the jokes about her being poor advertisement for her diner. She was so thin her white starched apron nearly went around her twice.

"Nice to see you, Bri." Rosie handed them each a menu, her gaze steady on Rafe. "Who's your friend?"

Bri raised her eyebrows in feigned surprise. "You mean you don't know?"

Her painted red lips curved in a mischievous grin. "Actually, I do. Peggy Sue just called."

Bri choked back a laugh.

Rafe gave Rosie a polite smile and then focused on the menu. It was difficult to tell if he understood what had happened. Maybe he purposely ignored her because the attention embarrassed him. Doubtful. More likely he was so used to women fawning over him, it didn't faze him.

Rosie narrowed her gaze under too much blue eye shadow. "So, you're a real honest-to-goodness sheikh, huh?"

He looked up, only a ghost of a smile playing about his lips, amusement glittering in his eyes. "That is what my parents tell me."

Rosie chuckled and glanced over her shoulder. "You hear that, Pearl? This one's got himself a sense of humor." She brought her gaze back to Rafe. "We had one stop by here and you could have sworn he had a corncob stuck up his—"

Bri noisily cleared her throat. "What's your special? I hope you have cobbler today."

"Peach." Rosie removed the pencil from behind her ear and pulled a notepad out of her apron pocket. "The lunch special was meat loaf. But we may be out." She craned her neck toward the kitchen. "Hey, Shortie, we got any meat loaf left?"

At the shrill way she yelled at her cook, Bri cringed and glanced at Rafe for his reaction. None. Not even a blink of an eye. He had one heck of a poker face.

God only knew what he was thinking. It had taken her quite a while to get used to the people around here. Most of them were nice, hardworking folks with hearts bigger than the Grand Canyon, but Bri was used to a more subdued New England environment where people tended to stick to themselves and certainly not try to break the sound barrier.

She also knew that it took just as long for the people around Bridle to warm up to her. They'd mistaken her shy reserve for snobbery. Jessica had been kind enough to explain in her oh-so-tactful way.

Bri smiled at the memory.

"Sorry, no meat loaf. The chicken-fried steak is mighty tasty, though."

She looked at Rafe. He was watching her, his dark eyes maddeningly unreadable. She swallowed and glanced around. All eyes were on them. "I'll just have the peach cobbler and coffee."

"You got it, sugar." Rosie scribbled the order on her notepad. "And you, Your Highness?"

One side of Rafe's mouth lifted, but he kept his gaze on Bri. "What would you recommend?"

"Ever had chili or barbecue?"

He frowned. "I do not believe so. What are these dishes?"

"Hell's bells, Bri, it took that boring New England pallet of yours nearly a year to get used to my chili." Rosie shook her head with disapproval. "You still won't touch barbecue sauce. What makes you think His Highness here would like either of those?"

Bri blushed. "That doesn't mean he wouldn't like it." Reluctantly she met his eyes. Expecting annoyance, she found amusement. "Allie likes kind of spicy dishes. I figured you might."

"I will try this chili." He handed Rosie the menu. "And iced tea."

She raised skeptical eyebrows. "Okay. I'll bring on the corn bread with it."

As soon as Rosie left, Rafe brought his gaze back to Bri. "Do you like living here?"

The question startled her. She didn't know what she'd expected him to say but it wasn't that. "Of course. Cord is here, and I've made some friends and— Why do you ask?"

"You seem different from these people."

"They're nice folks."

"My observation was not meant as a criticism."

She plucked at the paper napkin. "I know. I'm sorry. It's just that it did take me a while to get used to their ways. They're very open, friendly people."

"And they thought you were an ice princess."

She stiffened. "Is that your opinion?"

"No, Brianna." He smiled and lightly touched the back of her hand. "I think you are a kind, intelligent, beautiful young lady who knows when to hold her tongue."

Bri's heart lurched. "You don't know that."

"Ah, but as my sister has spoken of me, she has had much to say about you, as well." He shrugged. "And of course there are some things a man knows without counsel."

Kind. Beautiful. Intelligent. He thought she was all those things? She wasn't sure what the "holding her tongue" remark meant, but she'd give him the benefit of the doubt. She glanced toward the kitchen, hoping like crazy that Rosie would suddenly appear with their drinks and save Bri from having to respond.

The next best thing happened. The door to the diner

opened. Amanda Jenkins walked in. Bridle's blond bombshell.

She had a figure that made grown men weep and depressed the heck out of every woman south of Dallas.

Including Bri. Although she'd never paid too much attention before now, but once Rafe turned around and got a load of her...

"Hi, y'all." On her way to the counter, Amanda smiled at everyone in a broad all-encompassing way. But when her gaze fell on Rafe, she blinked and slowed. "Afternoon, Brianna," she said, her curious eyes staying on Rafe.

Be careful what you wish for, Aunt Elaine had said often. Bri fully understood now. She'd asked for a darn distraction. "Hello, Amanda."

Rafe glanced at her, smiled politely and then returned his attention to Bri.

She sat up a little straighter. Was the man blind? Everyone gave Amanda second and third looks. Even women and children.

"This evening, do you have any plans?" he asked, his concentration on her so absolute, it made Bri heady. She barely noticed Amanda had wandered off.

"Not exactly."

"Good."

"Why?"

"Tonight we have a date."

Startled, Bri bumped her silverware, sending her fork clanging to the floor and netting everyone's attention. When she started to pick it up, Rafe grasped her hand.

Under a dozen pairs of watchful eyes, still holding her hand, he leaned across the table and whispered, "I overheard you talking to Peggy Sue. Tonight I will teach you to dance."

Chapter Six

Bri flipped through the collection of CDs, her hands still shaking since lunch yesterday. That their dance lesson had been preempted last night by a phone call from Dallas had been both a blessing and a curse. The brief respite had turned into a sleepless night.

Of course, if she truly wanted to put an end to the evening before it started, she could play an Alan Jackson or Garth Brooks CD. She'd like to see Rafe try and show her how to two-step or line dance. Assuming he'd even heard of the western dance steps.

The real truth was that she could have refused, told him she wasn't interested in dance lessons from him or anyone. But she couldn't. She wanted his touch. She wanted to feel his arms around her.

Hearing something behind her in the den, she spun around.

Rafe had dragged the tan leather armchair closer to the fireplace. He straightened and surveyed the area. "This should be enough room."

They'd chosen the den because it was a spacious room that opened up to the kitchen and tiled foyer.

She thought they had plenty of room before he'd re-arranged the furniture. "What are we going to do, the tango?"

He smiled. "Among other things."

"I meant that as a joke," she muttered and turned back to the collection of CDs, her pulse beginning to race out of control. He was just a man. No different than Cord. He was Allie's brother, for goodness' sakes.

He walked up behind her, put a hand on her waist and she nearly melted into a puddle. "Ready?" he asked, his mouth close to her ear, his warm breath teasing her skin.

"Are you sure you aren't too busy? Because I really don't need to—"

He touched the other side of her waist and turned her to face him. "I am not too busy."

She held her breath. He was much too close, his dark eyes holding her gaze captive. How could she think straight? "I haven't chosen the music yet."

"I will help you decide." He let her go, but stood shoulder to shoulder with her while he flipped through the CDs. "You have quite an eclectic collection."

"They're mostly Cord's."

"Do you not like music?"

"I love music." She just didn't have many CDs of her own. "When I moved in, Cord already had all these and..." She shrugged, wondering why she hadn't added artists that suited her taste more.

She'd been so grateful to be recognized by Cord, and then taken into the family home, that in many ways she'd been afraid to rock the boat, to change the status quo. And now that Allie was the official woman of the house…

Bri couldn't go there. The thought was too depressing. Anyway, Cord had made her feel instantly welcome. She could have bought a hundred CDs, painted her room a different color, changed the kitchen wallpaper, he wouldn't have said a word. Her own insecurity was the problem. But still…

"I have said something wrong?" Rafe looked at her with concern in his dark eyes.

"No, nothing." She stared at a picture of Tim McGraw. "I'm just indecisive."

"How about this?" He withdrew a Celine Dion.

Her songs were all slow, of course, and Bri's heart skipped a beat. "Fine."

"Do not look so nervous. I am a very good teacher."

Anxious for a distraction, she took the CD from him and slid it in the player. The first song started, and when she turned around, he held his arms open to her. She barely suppressed a shiver and then moved forward.

"Relax, Brianna," he said, his voice low and close as he slid one arm around her waist. "Give me your hand."

"Oh." She'd been standing stiff, like a statue, except her heart was ready to race out of her chest.

"Here." Instead of taking her hand, he turned her around and started to knead the coiled muscles at the base of her neck and around her shoulders. "You are too tense."

Bri briefly closed her eyes. He had strong hands

and he knew just how much pressure to use. If she could get past the fact that it was *him* touching her, the massage would feel really good.

"You are supposed to be relaxing not tensing. Take a couple of deep breaths." He pushed his thumbs down either side of her backbone all the way to her waist and then back up again.

In spite of herself, her head began to drop forward. Her knees went a little boneless.

"That's it." He cupped her nape and worked the muscles there.

She'd never had a massage before and she decided she could get used to the pampering very easily. She'd almost forgotten whose hands performed all that magic.

"Perhaps you should lie down."

She tensed again. "Excuse me?"

"If you were to take off your shirt and lie on your stomach, I could give you a proper massage."

She turned to look at him. He seemed perfectly serious.

"Take off my shirt?"

He shrugged. "I would only see your back."

She moved away from him. Not because she was offended but amazingly, because she was tempted. The thought of his palms on her bare skin... "Where on earth did you learn to do a massage?"

"I have a masseur on staff at home. I simply did to you what he does to me. I may not be as good as Kahrim, but I try."

She averted her eyes, afraid she'd see laughter in his. This was all so casual to him and she was dying inside. She cleared her throat. "Let's get back to the dance lesson."

He gave another small shrug. "Of course."

"Shall I start the song over?"

"If you wish."

"You're the instructor."

At her unintended petulant tone, he laughed. "Leave the music, Brianna. Come."

She moved into his open arms, a little less nervous this time. Although why she should be more relaxed she had no idea. Maybe it was the massage. Or maybe the patience in his voice put her at ease, and his gentle touch. Of course, he was very practiced with women. Allie hadn't had to tell her that much.

Bri had seen firsthand how his casual charm sneaked up and disarmed the unsuspecting female. Never would she have guessed Peggy Sue, grandmother of four, would have reacted the way she had yesterday. And the envy on Amanda's face still made Bri giddy. Even Rosie hadn't quite been herself.

Bri sighed. Not to mention her own pitiful reaction to his attention. Which was really crazy. Rafe dated beautiful, sophisticated women. While he was in Bridle and Allie was away, Bri was his only playmate, so to speak. She wasn't special. Only available. And she best not forget it.

"You must stand closer." He put pressure on her lower back and she moved against him. "Your hand?"

Quickly she pressed her palm to his, embarrassed that she hadn't been paying attention, that she'd been too busy daydreaming about him.

"Now, I will go slowly. You follow my feet."

She nodded without looking up.

"Ready?"

"Ready."

He moved back and she stepped on his right foot. Her gaze flew to his face. "Sorry."

He didn't even blink. "No problem. We will try again. More slowly this time."

"Okay." She took a quick breath. What a klutz! If she stepped on his foot again she'd just die.

Again he stepped back, and she stumbled into him. His arms tightened around her.

"Maybe this isn't such a good idea." She tried to free herself but he held her closer still.

"If I did not know better, I would think you were afraid of me." His face only inches away, his gaze fell to her lips.

Involuntarily, she moistened them.

His nostrils flared slightly, and heat flamed in her belly, filled her chest, spread up her neck and into her cheeks. She willed him to kiss her. Right now. Before either of them realized how foolish that would be.

Finally he raised his gaze to meet her eyes. But instead of a kiss, he said, "That offer of a massage is still open."

What was he asking her? She felt so confused. So out of her league. Surely there was a clever answer, something witty and flip. "Um…I, um…I'm okay. Just clumsy."

"You are a very graceful woman. In everything you do." He pushed back a stray tendril of hair, the back of his knuckles brushing her cheek. "Even the way you mount a horse or get into a car. You are not clumsy. You are nervous. I wish I understood why.''

The song has stopped and Celine was halfway through the next one. But they stood there, facing each other, his expression one of concern, her insides as jittery as a bowl of Jell-O.

''You,'' Bri blurted. ''You make me nervous.''

His eyebrows lifted in genuine surprise. ''Me? What have I done?''

A cursed and inevitable blush flooded her face. ''I don't know. Nothing, really.''

He guided her chin back when she tried to look away. ''You have nothing to fear from me.''

''I know that.'' She pulled back, out of his reach, and crossed her arms over her chest. Darn her big mouth.

He walked away from her, and her heart sank. Not that she wanted his attention, but obviously she'd offended him. But he only went to the CD player and turned down the volume. ''Come.'' He took her hand and she let him lead her to the middle of the den. ''We need to talk.''

Oh, no. She perched gingerly on the edge of the couch. It wasn't as if she thought she'd have to make a run for it, but still...

Her unease clearly did not please him. His mouth drew into a tight line as he sat at the other end of the couch and eyed her poised-for-flight position.

She took a deep breath and tried to relax. She was being ridiculous. ''This doesn't have anything to do with you,'' she said, and then shrugged. ''Not exactly.''

"Of course it does. I have been too pushy."

"Oh, no. I-it's me. Really. I don't do well around strangers." Handsome men, in particular, but she needn't be that honest.

His eyebrows went together in disbelief. "Why?"

"I don't know. I guess that's just the way I'm wired."

"You were quite comfortable in town yesterday."

"I know those people."

He frowned thoughtfully. "Perhaps it was wrong for me to stay here with you."

"No." She nearly reached for his hand but drew back, though her attempt clearly didn't go unnoticed. "Please. I don't want to make you uncomfortable." She swallowed, searching for the right words. "You know, it's not every day a girl meets a real-life sheikh."

His frown deepened. He didn't get it. "That is merely a title. I am a man, like any other."

Oh, boy, was he wrong. She hesitated for a moment, and considered how much she should censor herself. "Frankly, that's baloney."

One eyebrow went up.

"That basically means I don't believe that's true."

"I am familiar with the term. It is your attitude that surprises me."

She willed herself not to blush…a futile effort. Still, she wouldn't back down. "You aren't like everyone else. While you're staying here, it may appear that way. But you can't possibly think the general public has the same opportunities or perspective as you do."

The amusement in his eyes annoyed her. "But nor do they have the same responsibilities."

"True," she conceded, knowing from Allie that Rafe took helping his country very seriously. "But the privileges must outweigh the demands."

"Perhaps."

"How did you get here?"

"To Texas?"

She nodded, feeling more comfortable now that the topic was about him.

"A jet, of course."

"A personal jet. Your jet."

He didn't look amused now. "Yes."

"How many people do you know—" She rolled her eyes. "Never mind. Silly question. Common people don't own their own jets. They don't travel halfway across the world just to buy horses."

"Arabians."

At his indignation, she smiled. "Excuse me. I stand corrected."

"It is not a crime to acquire wealth. In fact, most people in this country prize such a notion."

"Please don't be defensive. I'm not criticizing you. I'm merely pointing out the difference between you and the average person."

Rafe understood most women. Their needs were simple and universal. He did not understand Brianna. "And because of all this, I make you uncomfortable?"

She blinked. "Well, there's a little more to it."

"Explain."

She drew in her lower lip. A habit she had of displaying her uncertainty he found most appealing. "This is another small example."

He exhaled his frustration. She spoke in riddles.

"When you order someone to do something, it wouldn't occur to you that they wouldn't obey."

He hesitated, trying to interpret her assertion. "I asked you to explain. That was not an order."

"Granted, but am I right?"

"I do not give orders. I do on occasion give guidance."

Her lips curved in a most aggravating smile. "Okay," she said, her voice contradicting the word.

"I am a businessman. Not unlike an American employer, my expertise in certain areas puts me in a position of power."

"I understand."

But she didn't, he was certain. She viewed him as someone the Americans read about in their vile tabloids, like the sultan who had been photographed in a compromising position with a Swedish actress.

The only redeeming feature of this conversation was that she no longer seemed nervous. Was it because the focus had shifted to him? He shook his head. She thought he was different from other men, yet it was she who was different. She did not behave at all like most beautiful women he knew.

At first he believed that perhaps she was being artfully coy, an act to lure him. But to the dismay of his ego, she seemed genuinely anxious to keep her distance. Ironically, her reticence fueled his interest. Like a hound in search of a fox, he was compelled to the chase.

Perhaps that was why he was so captivated with her. Her reserve intrigued him, tempted him. He could not remember a woman ever igniting such obsessive thoughts. Preparing for the Dallas meeting should be occupying his time. Not shadowing Brianna.

He forced himself to remember she was barely twenty-three, and that he had given Cord his word he would watch over her. Only harmless flirting could transpire. And even that was a risk.

"I'm sorry I've upset you."

He looked into her clear blue eyes and saw earnest regret. "You have not upset me in the least."

"Right."

"Brianna, you are guilty only of provoking some thought. Nothing more."

Curiosity lit her eyes, but she refrained from asking the question. "You sure have been thinking a long time."

He laughed. "Yes, too long." He stood and held out a hand. "Shall we dance?"

"I've been thinking, too, and I don't—"

He took her hand and pulled her to her feet before she could renege. "We have the entire evening to convince your feet to cooperate."

She made a face. "Thanks for the reminder."

"Think nothing of it."

She smiled. "I'm glad I could teach you a new phrase."

"See?" He led her to the middle of the clear area. "We teach each other new things."

Her smile broadened, and this time when he put his arms around her she was much more relaxed. He held her close, the welcome feel of her breasts pressed to his chest making him question his sanity.

Her hair smelled of fresh spring rain, clean and pure, and its pale silkiness filled him with such foolish desire he thought perhaps he truly was going insane. What spell had this woman cast on him that he would follow her into town and into dress shops like an old woman?

Maybe it was because she was forbidden fruit that he had this craving to touch her, to take her to his bed. Of course he would not. He would settle for the pleasure of having her body pressed to his while they danced.

He moved his hand down her back and rested it just above the swell of her buttocks. She shifted and he retreated slightly, fearing his body's physical reaction. Just as he suspected, she was graceful on her feet. Now that she was more relaxed, she followed his lead with little effort.

"You are doing very well," he whispered in her ear, and she shivered in his arms. And then she stumbled.

"We can't talk about it or I'll falter."

"And I will be here to catch you."

She stiffened and he wondered what he had said that was so wrong. "I don't think they'll be doing too much slow dancing next Saturday."

"Will there be both men and women there?"

She drew her head back and looked at him as if he had gone insane. "Of course."

"Then there will be slow dancing."

She laughed, and he pulled her close again, enjoying the feel of her warm breath on his throat, the sweet sound of her laughter. He lightly kissed the top of her head and inhaled her womanly scent.

"I think you may have been making sport of me."

She looked up at him, her beautiful eyes wide and serious. "How do you mean?"

"You are no novice at dancing. You move like a gentle wind."

A misstep landed her on his right foot. "Thank you for breaking my concentration," she said, and the pink immediately bloomed in her cheeks.

"There is no need to concentrate. Just follow me." Their eyes met. "I will not lead you astray."

"And what if I don't have such a good partner next Saturday?"

The sudden thought of her in another man's arms made him crazy. "I will be there to rescue you."

Annoyance flickered in her gaze. "I don't need a chaperon."

He shrugged and urged her to lay her head on his shoulder. Her face was too close, her full pink lips too tempting. The desire to kiss her battled his common sense. "It is merely an excuse."

She drew her head back again to look at him. "An excuse for what?"

"To be with you."

She blinked. "You're teasing me."

"Not in the least."

She laid her head on his shoulder again, clearly to avoid his gaze. The rapid pounding of her heart against his chest told him more than her expression could.

His admission had been foolish, perhaps even dangerous. What had he hoped to gain? This impulsive nonsense was most unlike him. Not only foolish but also undignified.

Slowly she lifted her head and met his gaze. His defenses crumbled. The desire in her eyes as she moistened her lips was his final undoing. They stopped dancing, and when he lowered his head, she lifted her chin to meet him.

The shrill sound of the telephone was like a dousing of cold water. She jumped back, her face a mask of confusion. And then she hurried to answer it.

She picked up the receiver and greeted the caller with a shaky hello, and when she heard the news about Rafe's foal her heart sank. Fate sure didn't want anything to happen between her and Rafe. As she turned to him, she wondered if she could change fate…if only for one night.

Chapter Seven

"Are we too late?" Bri rushed into the stables ahead of Rafe. Anyone would think this was her foal about to be born.

She didn't care. The distraction was perfect.

She'd almost kissed Rafe.

Oh, God, she couldn't think about that right now.

Alex Coleman, the developer of the breeding program for the Desert Rose, looked up from his crouched position beside Anastasia in the foaling stall. "No, but I think we're getting close. She's been restless for the past two hours and there's a prominent drop to her belly. Her ribs are pretty well-sprung and her milk veins are enlarged. Hannah thinks she'll foal within an hour."

Anastasia kicked her hind legs and whimpered. She had the saddest look in her liquid brown eyes. Rafe lowered himself beside her to stroke her neck and whisper words Bri didn't understand. They were in his language but the soothing tone was universal. The mare looked at him with trust and pressed her nose against his hand.

"The next time she stands I've got to wrap her tail," Alex said to Rafe. "I'll need that Ace bandage over there."

Rafe immediately responded, grabbing the package off the table near the stall door and tearing it open.

Bri rubbed her palms down the front of her jeans. She'd never been to anything like this before. She hoped she didn't do anything stupid like pass out. In high school she couldn't sit through a film on human birth. She'd gotten so queasy she had to make a bee-line out of the classroom.

"Where's Hannah?" Maybe she could make herself useful elsewhere.

Alex used his chin to point toward the back of the stables where they had an infirmary. "Getting more warm towels."

"I'll go see if I can help." That sounded lame but the men were too busy comforting Anastasia to notice.

Bri lingered for a moment, watching Rafe, impressed with the way he helped calm the mare. The animal was damp with sweat and drool but he seemed unconcerned for his clothes or anything. A few days ago this may have amazed her. Not now. He was far more gentle and down-to-earth than she had expected.

He constantly surprised and disarmed her. She wanted to kiss him. Right now. But of course, she wouldn't.

A clattering sound from the back of the stables brought her to her senses and she hurried to find Alex's wife. Hannah was a vet and she cared for most of the horses at the Desert Rose. Bri didn't know her all that well but what she knew she liked a lot.

"Hey." Hannah looked up from the tray equipped with rolled cotton, Betadine and iodine. "You got here fast." She used the back of her arm to wipe away the honey-blond hair that had escaped her ponytail and clung to her flushed face. "Good thing. She's in the imminent parturition stage. Shouldn't be long now."

"I'm glad you called. Rafe is with Alex and Anastasia."

"Was she up or down when you left?"

"Down," Bri said, and Hannah frowned with concern. "Alex said he'd bandage her tail as soon as she got up again. Rafe is helping him."

"Rafe know anything about the birthing process?"

Bri shrugged. "All I know is he really wanted to be here. He would've been disappointed if he'd missed it. That's why he stuck around." Bri grabbed a wet towel before it fell off the counter when Hannah moved the tray. "Besides, Anastasia seems awfully glad he's here. He's very patient and gentle and he's the most—"

Hannah gave her a funny look.

Bri swallowed, wondering what she'd said that had Hannah trying to hide a smile. "Not that you and Alex aren't doing a good job. Of course you are, but—what?"

Hannah laughed. "Nothing. I'm just glad to see you two are getting along."

Bri frowned. That was an odd remark. Hannah didn't really know him as far as Bri was aware.

The woman grabbed a couple of pairs of latex gloves and handed one pair to Bri. "I left a message for Jessie. She wanted to be here, too."

Darn it. That's what the curious look was about. Jessie obviously had said something about Rafe. No telling what, knowing Jessie. Heat spread across Bri's face, but Hannah had already switched her attention to stacking clean towels.

Bri envied the vet. She knew Hannah had once been shy and uncertain, much like Bri, but she hadn't let that obstacle stop her. She'd gone to veterinarian school and made something of herself, and now she was married to Alex, who was a terrific guy, and they had twin sons.

"Bri, do me a favor. Grab another pair of gloves for Jessie."

She did as she was asked, only now considering the pair Hannah had given her. Her stomach did a little flip-flop. "Um, what am I supposed to do with these?"

"Wear them?"

"I know that, but why? I mean, I want to help and all, but I don't have to touch anything icky, do I?"

Hannah chuckled. "Are you the squeamish type?"

"Guilty."

"Don't worry. The gloves are for just in case. Anastasia will be doing all the work and she won't want any interference." Hannah lifted the tray, and Bri grabbed the stack of towels. "You can stand in the cheering section by her head. You won't see anything *icky* until the foal makes an appearance.''

Bri felt like an idiot. She thought she'd be okay, but even the odor of the swabs and iodine had started to get to her. "You're probably wondering why I even came.''

"Let me tell you…Jessie isn't exactly a pillar of strength when it involves anything to do with bodily fluids.'' Hannah smiled and bumped her affectionately with her shoulder. "Don't worry about it. Most people can't stomach a live birth. Unless it's their own baby, of course. And even then, some new fathers…well, it's not pretty.'' She grinned. "Come on. Let's go rescue the guys.''

Feeling marginally better, Bri followed her back to Anastasia's stall. Rafe and Alex had managed to wrap the mare's tail and she was starting to go down again. Rafe stayed with her, trying to soothe the poor thing who continued to whimper, her wrapped tail flicking like crazy.

"How's it going?'' Hannah asked as she set the tray on a small portable table.

"She's hanging in there,'' Alex said, "but I hope junior decides to come out soon. The poor girl's miserable.''

Hannah crouched down beside her husband and gently examined the mare's udder. "You've done this before, Anastasia. You can do it again.'' She stroked the mare's neck, letting her hand linger for a moment. "Her pulse rate is fast but good. She's started to dilate. It should be any minute now.''

Bri stood off to the side, her hands tightly clasped together. She felt like excess baggage. What could she do to help? Not fainting would be good. Oh, God, she'd die of embarrassment.

"Bri? I bet the guys could use some water." There was sympathy and understanding in Hannah's eyes. "Mind getting a few bottles out of the fridge?"

"Sure. In the infirmary?"

Hannah nodded. "They should be cold by now."

Rafe slowly got to his feet, obviously stiff from crouching. "I will go with you. I need to exercise my legs."

Bri really wished he wouldn't. Being alone with him would make her think of their almost kiss and she was already nervous enough. She darted a look at Hannah who watched Rafe with avid interest. When her gaze swung back to Bri's, Hannah gave her a knowing smile, and then focused on Anastasia.

Although what Hannah thought she knew, Bri had no idea. Well, that wasn't quite accurate...she had *some* idea. Darn Jessie, this was all her fault.

"I do not think the mare will give birth in the next minute."

At the teasing in Rafe's voice, Bri realized that she'd been practically jogging ahead of him. The implication in Hannah's smile had made her adrenaline go haywire. She slowed down and Rafe paced alongside her.

"Hannah did say it could be any minute."

"I doubt we will miss anything by walking instead of running."

"I wasn't running." She sighed. What did it matter?

He stretched his neck to the side, and massaged the muscle at the top of his thigh. "I am sadly out of shape."

"Right."

His left eyebrow went up. "You try crouching that long. It is not easy to move suddenly."

"That's my point—" She decided to let the matter drop. Short of explaining that she thought he was in pretty fine shape, darn near perfect, there'd be no satisfying conclusion.

They arrived at the infirmary and he stopped her before she opened the fridge. "I have made you uncomfortable. For that I am truly sorry."

She frowned, confused. "No, you haven't."

"Back at the Flying Ace, I was not the gentleman I should have been."

Oh, God. Why did he have to bring that up? "Nothing happened. I don't know what you're talking about." She ducked around him to open the refrigerator door.

"You are acting oddly. It is my fault."

She shook her head and sighed. "It's not you." That was half-true. "I—um, the whole birthing thing—" Did she really want to admit this? She cleared her throat. "I get a little queasy over the sight of blood." She wrinkled her nose. "And other such things."

Understanding registered in his face. "But you came anyway."

She shrugged. "Of course. This is a special occasion."

"You are very brave."

"Yeah, right."

"You face your fears. Is that not bravery?"

She hesitated, thinking about it for a moment. "You haven't seen my reaction yet. At the first sight of the foal, I'm liable to fall flat on my face."

"My point precisely." He lifted a hand and brushed her cheek.

She swallowed and cast a nervous glance toward the open infirmary door.

He retreated. "You are aware of the possible consequences, yet you do not let your fear stop you. That defines bravery. You have my admiration."

She didn't know what to say. His words, the sincerity in his eyes, they made her knees weak. "Thank you. I would never have seen it that way."

"Because you are also modest." He murmured something in his own language. "You both delight and baffle me."

A shiver of pleasure nearly swept her off her feet, and she struggled to think, to speak.

"We had better get the water before Anastasia starts without us."

Her hand still rested on the refrigerator door handle and with a start, she finally opened it.

With a faint smile, he reached in and grabbed three bottles of Evian. "When she starts to push the foal out, stand by the mare's head."

"Exactly what I'm planning to do." She snatched two more bottles of water.

"If you get light-headed, signal to me."

"I'll be fine."

"Yes, you will." He closed the door. "I will make certain of it."

RAFE WATCHED BRIANNA out of the corner of his eye. She had grown pale and he could see her chest rise and fall with the deep calming breaths she took as she huddled in the corner. She was a remarkable woman with estimable courage.

Someday he hoped to find a woman such as her, one who could sit beside him when he stepped up to rule Munir. She would be a woman who was his own kind.

He had never thought much about marriage. He knew only that he was expected to provide the royal family with an heir, which made marriage inevitable. If he had had any feelings on the subject at all, it was resignation. But he had been in no hurry. He had many willing companions to satisfy his physical needs in the meantime.

So why was unease building inside him like an active volcano, simmering to eventual eruption? Resentment had haunted his dreams last night. A general discontent governed his mood this morning.

This was a happy occasion. A miracle was about to take place. But something gnawing inside him prevented his total enjoyment.

Brianna was of course the problem. His preoccupation with her had thrown him off-kilter. With every surprise she presented him, he stumbled further off balance. The entire matter was most infuriating. Yet the feeling of helplessness persisted.

"I'm not too late, am I?" Jessica rushed into the stables, her red hair flying wildly about her face. "I just got the message."

Anastasia brayed pitifully as her upper lips curled and she bared her gums.

"Actually, you're right on time," Hannah said, her gaze trained on the mare. "She's having another contraction. Oh, good, her water just broke. Okay, everyone, you all need to stand back."

Bri inched back farther into the corner, hugging herself and nibbling at her lower lip.

Jessica went to join her.

Alex stayed near Hannah, and Rafe moved back a few feet, but stayed in a position to see the foal come into the world.

"Good girl, Anastasia, good girl," Hannah cooed softly as she watched for the foal. "You can do it. It'll all be over soon."

All was silent for several moments before Anastasia's heavy breathing and quiet whimpers rent the air. And then the miracle unfolded.

Rafe stared in fascination as the hooves emerged. He inhaled deeply. Another push and he could see the whole front end of the foal.

Amazing.

Hannah continued to speak to the mare. He paid

no attention until her voice rose slightly. Something was wrong.

"The hooves didn't break the amniotic sac. It's not a big deal," she said calmly. "But I'm going to have to tear it."

No one said a word. They all watched in silence as she tore the sac open and the foal's head and shoulders appeared. It opened its eyes.

Brianna stepped closer, her eyes wide and glistening with emotion. "Oh my God." She put a hand to her throat. "This is incredible."

"Are you okay?" Rafe whispered.

"What?" She looked at him, her expression dazed.

"Do you feel faint?"

Surprise flickered in her eyes, as if she had forgotten she was prone to queasiness, and then she shook her head and turned back to focus on the foal.

"Come." He took her hand and urged her to stand beside him where she would have a better view of the baby.

She readily complied, catching him off guard when she stood so close their thighs and shoulders touched. He fought the urge to slip an arm around her. The gesture, no matter how innocent or casual, would embarrass her in front of the others.

He contented himself with standing close, inhaling her scent while they shared the miracle of the foal's birth.

"What are you naming him?" she whispered.

"Him? You are so sure it is not a filly?"

"Well, I didn't look." She blushed.

Hannah grinned over her shoulder. "You're going to have to buy cigars with blue ribbons around them."

Rafe frowned. He had no idea what she meant.

Brianna laughed. "She's trying to tell you it's a boy."

"Cigars?"

"It's an American custom for the father to pass out cigars when his baby is born."

"Ah. I see." He stared at the excitement in Brianna's eyes. He could watch her all night.

"Easy, boy." Hannah's voice drew his attention. She helped the foal to his feet, supporting him as he tried to stand on his own. "That's it."

Black as midnight, he looked like such a gangly creature right now, but Rafe knew he would grow into a fine Arabian just like his father. And Rafe would watch him develop, experience the wonder of his growth.

An odd pang of longing lodged itself in his chest, a longing for a child of his own. The idea was so startling, he stepped back.

Brianna gave him a curious look. "Are you okay?"

"Of course." He stared at the colt. "What would you name him?"

She pursed her lips. "I'm not sure. I'd have to think about it."

"Yes, think about it, and then we will decide together."

She blinked. "Naming a horse is very serious around here, especially if he's going to be shown."

"I agree. The name should be given grave consideration."

"No, I mean, you should be the one who names him. Something that has meaning for you." She looked uncomfortable suddenly, and crossed her arms over her chest in a protective manner.

"Brianna—"

"Can you believe this?" Jessica positioned herself alongside them for a better look at the foal. "This is probably the tenth or eleventh birth I've seen and it amazes me every time."

"I've never seen anything like it before." Brianna's gaze went back to Hannah and the still-struggling foal. "I didn't even know I could make it to the end."

The foal would make it to his feet and then his skinny legs would wobble and he would go back down. But he was a resilient creature and continued trying to stand, and with Hannah's help managed to stay up for almost a minute.

For the next half hour, they all watched in silence until he finally stayed on his feet by himself. Anastasia patiently waited for her offspring to discover how to nurse, and then she was rewarded with a warm bran mash Alex put in front of her.

Hannah stood back, smiling. "I think it's time we left these two to bond."

Brianna made a soft sound of disappointment. Rafe furtively reached for her hand and gave it a squeeze. In return she gave him a shy smile. Everyone else's eyes were on the colt, so he pulled her closer.

She leaned into him, her head nearly resting on his shoulder. He wanted to hold her closer still, kiss her and tell her how much it meant to have shared this experience with her. He wanted to whisper words of seduction that would land her in his bed tonight.

Hannah and Alex backed up, giving them the signal it was time to leave. When Brianna did not move, Rafe slipped his arm around her and whispered, "We have to go."

She nodded and snuggled closer as they both turned to leave.

But at Jessica's surprised look, Brianna bolted ahead of him toward the truck.

Rafe did not try to stop her. She was better off running from him. He could promise her nothing. Better she kept running and never looked back.

Chapter Eight

Bri lounged in bed, yawning and staring at the ribbon of sunlight streaming in from under her bedroom shade. This was likely the latest she'd ever slept in. Even all those cold dreary New Hampshire winter mornings hadn't kept her in bed this long, but she didn't care.

She'd dreamed about Rafe and about the birth she'd witnessed last night, and she wasn't ready to let go. Reality would interfere soon enough. But for now, she replayed the dream where Rafe had scooped her up into his arms and carried her to his bed.

Not his bed here at the Flying Ace. In the dream his bedroom was in a large castle with lots of filmy curtains and scented candles. The bed had no ordinary mattress, either. It was like one huge feather pillow where he gently laid her in the middle. And then he'd begun to undress her, slowly, his face tender yet hungry as he bowed his head to kiss her, first on the lips, then on the throat and then her breasts...

She sighed, painfully aware it truly was just a

dream. Last night after they returned home, Rafe couldn't seem to get away from her fast enough.

He'd immediately withdrawn his cell phone from his pocket, murmured something about having business to take care of, and then disappeared into his room for the rest of the night. Fool that she was, she'd waited until midnight for him to emerge. He never did, and she finally went to bed with her dreams.

A loud knock made her jump. She sat up and stared at her closed door. That wasn't where the sound came from, was it?

Another knock. From outside?

Where was Rafe? Was he even home?

She grabbed her robe and pulled it on over her Tweety Bird nightshirt. If someone were at the front door they would have rung the bell. Besides, a knock that far away couldn't be heard in her room.

It was quiet when she stepped out into the hall. Rafe's bedroom door was open, which meant he was already up. She sniffed the air. It almost smelled like burnt coffee.

Another knock drew her attention to the patio doors. Jessica stood outside, a frustrated look on her face.

Bri hurried to the glass door and unlocked it.

Jessie sized her up as she came in. "Were you still in bed?"

Bri sighed and nodded. People around here got up at the crack of dawn.

"Alone?" Her gaze darted past Bri toward the hall. Bri glanced over her shoulder to make sure Rafe wasn't around to hear that remark. "Of course. Don't be silly."

"Oh, please." Jessie gave her the once-over. "You look this good when you first wake up? That's disgusting."

Bri's hand automatically went to her hair. She couldn't imagine what that mop looked like. And then a horrible thought occurred to her. "Is anything wrong with Anastasia or the colt?"

"Oh, no." Jessie waved a hand. "Mother and baby are doing just fine. I don't suppose you have some coffee made." She sniffed the air the way Bri had, although the odor wasn't so strong out here. "Forget I asked."

"I have no idea what that is." Bri went to the wet bar, suddenly desperate for a drink of water. "Rafe might have tried to make toast."

Jessie laughed. "Maybe he was going to bring you breakfast in bed."

"Very funny." She grabbed a pitcher out of the small fridge. "Want something to drink?"

"No, I want you to give me the scoop on what's happening around here."

"Nothing." Bri passed Jessie on the way to the couch and made a face when her friend pushed aside the front of her robe for a peek.

"Tweety Bird?" Jessie shook her head at the nightshirt. "Honey, we have to do something about this."

"I like this shirt." She sank to the couch, set her glass of water on the side table, and then tightened the belt to her robe. "Cord gave it to me for Christmas."

Jessie snorted. "Your brother hasn't realized you're all grown up. He'd probably like it just fine if you wore ruffles and pigtails." She took the tan leather armchair opposite Bri, curling her legs under her. "Now, tell me about Rafe."

Exasperated, Bri groaned. "There's not a blessed thing to tell."

"Oh, come on, even Hannah noticed how he looked at you, and she was slightly busy last night."

"You're wrong." Bri adamantly shook her head. "Not only is there nothing going on, but he hardly knows I exist."

"Are you kidding?"

"Oh, Jessie." Bri laughed. "I'm serious. Nothing is happening. Nada. Zip."

"Bri. The guy looks at you like he wants to eat you with a spoon."

Well, that was a new term. "I'm not even going to ask," she said, glancing nervously toward the kitchen and then down the hall. It occurred to her they shouldn't be talking so freely. "I don't know where he is, so please keep it down."

"Then fess up."

Bri groaned. "Okay, so he knows I exist, but last night had more to do with the foal being born and—what?"

Jessie gave her a mischievous smile. "Let's try another tactic. How do you feel about *him?*"

Bri's cheeks stung with heat. "He's Allie's brother. Cord's brother-in-law." She shrugged. "He's nice. What do you want me to say?"

Jessica sighed. "You are the most difficult woman

I know. We're supposed to talk about these things. You know, like makeup, hair…boys.''

Bri took another sip of water. That was the thing…she didn't know about girl talk. Aunt Elaine had discouraged her from having friends. She'd thought the high-school girls Bri had gone to school with were all tramps, and that they'd end up getting knocked up just like Bri's mother had.

That wasn't true. Most of the girls at Snow Mountain High were really nice, serious students. But it had been a whole lot easier for Bri to obey her aunt than make friends.

She looked at Jessie. Her first real friend. They had bonded rather quickly considering Bri's reticence, and she'd been kind and patient with Bri, helping her adjust to Bridle, even when half the town hadn't believed she was Cord's sister and the rumors flew fast and furious.

Yet Jessie had never uttered an unkind word about anyone in Bri's presence. No, that wasn't quite true. She'd had plenty to say about Nick before he'd become her husband. Bri smiled, thinking about how Jessie used to go into hour-long diatribes every time she'd had to go see Nick in Dallas for Desert Rose business.

"What?" Jessie leaned forward. "Tell me."

"I was thinking about you and Nick."

"Darn it, Bri. We're talking about you and Rafe." She narrowed her gaze. "What about me and Nick?"

"I was just remembering how much he irritated you before you got married."

"Ain't love grand?" She grinned. "Actually,

sometimes he still irritates me, but I love the making-up part. Now, quit changing the subject.''

Sighing, Bri drew her legs up under her bottom and adjusted her robe. Jessie was right. Friends talked about this sort of thing. ''The truth?'' She lowered her voice and took another brief reassuring look over her shoulder. ''I think he's extraordinarily handsome, very sexy, much nicer than I ever dreamed he'd be, and he has absolutely no interest in me.''

''Bri, are you crazy? That is so not true.''

''Let me clarify that…he may be interested phys-ically, just because I'm the only woman in the house, but I'm not his type. He thinks I'm too young for one thing, and I'm not sophisticated enough.''

Jessie frowned. ''How do you know that?''

''Because.''

''Well, that explains everything.'' Jessie rolled her eyes.

''Because he's had plenty of opportunity to kiss me and he hasn't even tried.'' She thought about the time they'd danced. He'd had an opportunity then, but hadn't taken it. ''That's why.''

''Have you?''

''Kissed him?''

''Yeah.'' Jessie shrugged a shoulder. ''Or even tried.''

''Right. Like I'm going to do that.'' She got up. She needed more water. Heck, she needed a Bloody Mary.

Jessie followed. ''Why not?''

''He'll think I'm a—''

''What?''

"I don't know."

"Bri, you've got to let him know you're interested."

"No, I don't." She poured another glass of water. "He was only waiting for the foal to be born. He'll probably leave tomorrow." The thought made her sick. She didn't want him to leave. Not before they…

Oh, God, she didn't know what she wanted.

Jessie touched her arm. "Hey, I think you're wrong about him not being interested. Cord probably told him he'd break his neck if even had a single thought about you."

"Cord wouldn't do that."

"Wanna bet? Why do you think none of the Desert Rose hands have asked you out?"

Bri's blood pressure soared. It was bad enough he'd told Rafe she was off-limits, but the hands, too? "He warned them off?"

"Not in so many words." Jessie shrugged. "He's a big brother. They do stuff like that, but that's not important here. You have to make a move to let Rafe know you're interested."

Bri muttered a curse. A word she had never in her life said before now. "I must be crazy," she whispered. "He could be somewhere in this house listening to everything we've said."

"We weren't talking loud enough, and if he were around we'd have heard him. Quit trying to change the subject."

Bri rubbed her eyes. She wanted to crawl back into bed and pull the covers over her head. And why not?

She hadn't taken an entire day off in months. Maybe she'd do just that...

"Okay, let's see." Jessie pursed her lips in concentration and ran a hand through her red hair. "What's your day like tomorrow? You have anything important to do?"

"Why?" Bri crossed her arms over her chest. She didn't like her friend's enthusiastic tone.

"You'll see." Jessica smiled as she headed for the door. "Uh, don't make any plans for tomorrow afternoon."

RAFE DID NOT SUFFER incompetence well. In himself or anyone else. He entered the kitchen through the back door and stared at the disaster he had created. The pan on the stove was probably burnt beyond repair. Of course, he would have it replaced, but that did not solve the problem of the impossible cheese omelette he had attempted.

He had cooked before. At Harvard after some of the fellows had teased him mercilessly about being spoiled and helpless. He quickly had learned to make scrambled eggs and toast and he had even successfully made pancakes once.

Perhaps he had been too distracted this morning, he thought as he set down the boxed food from Rosie's diner. Brianna was on his mind and he did not know how to rid himself of the obsession.

Brianna.

He swore to himself, hoping she had not yet awoken. She did not need to see this mess. He got down two plates and then unloaded the cartons of food Rosie's cook had prepared. All he had to do was figure out how to work the microwave.

"What on earth?"

Brianna's voice came from behind, and he again cursed to himself.

"Rafe?"

"Do not concern yourself. I will—" He turned around. Her hair was tousled, her legs bare under the short robe. He lost his train of thought.

Her expression turned wary and she tightened the belt of her robe. "Have you been in here all this time?"

"I just returned from—an errand." He blocked the view of the white cartons. "I made coffee."

Alarm flickered in her eyes. "How nice. Thank you." Her gaze scanned the splattered counters and the pair of charred pot holders. "I think I'll go grab a shower first."

He nodded, anxious to dispose of the food cartons. "And then we will have breakfast together."

"Sure." Her smile forced, she cast a final glance around the kitchen.

He waited for her to leave before he finished preparing their breakfast. His plan to serve her in bed was obviously defunct. But he could still salvage the meal. They would eat in the dining room where they did not have to view the havoc he had created.

The flowers. He had forgotten them in the truck.

Quickly he transferred the food to the plates, and then carried them into the dining room. Back in Munir, there were chafing dishes on the long buffet in the dining room from which the servants served their meals. That way the food never grew cold.

Here, Brianna tended to all the mundane tasks. He knew they had a housekeeper and that she was away, but in the interim, Brianna never complained, merely made sure the household ran smoothly. Another surprise for a woman of such beauty.

Today she would wait on no one, including him. He would serve her breakfast…he glanced at the clock. It was closer to lunch, which made his plan all the more perfect.

He finished arranging the food that needed no heating on the table, and set apart the one dish that had to be microwaved. And then he went to the truck for the flowers. They were not as fresh as they should be and he realized he should have put them in water as soon as he had remembered them.

The morning's ordeal had been most enlightening. Not particularly pleasant, but it made him realize how much Brianna had been right. His needs were always met before they emerged. Food was always warm and plentiful, his laundered clothes ready and waiting, and today had been the first time he had driven himself in years.

This was the way most people lived. How quickly he forgot. The idea shamed him. Yet he did not apologize for the privileged life to which he had been born. Along with it came responsibilities. But how much wiser he was to see the other side of life.

He sniffed the blistered air. Not that he wished to extend the experience. Admittedly he would pay handsomely for someone else to clean up the mess.

He knew Brianna would do it without complaint. Glancing around at the soiled pots and pans, the crusted spills, he was tempted to let her.

Sighing with disgust, he rolled up his sleeves.

BRI TOOK the fastest shower in history, blow-dried her hair only halfway and then climbed into a pair of tight faded jeans she should have thrown away weeks ago.

What the heck was Rafe up to? Along with the smell of burnt toast, she'd also smelled real food. Plus, he had acted a little funny. Of course, that was probably just about the mess.

She ran a brush through her hair, leaving it down so it would finish drying on its own. If it got frizzy or wavy, she could put it up later. She almost forgot to apply mascara, the only makeup she wore to hide her blond lashes.

She returned to the kitchen being extra quiet, hoping to sneak up on him. If he was up to no good, she wanted to find out on her own terms.

To her surprise, the kitchen was partially clean. The pots and pans were stacked in the sink and the stove and counters thoroughly wiped down. A few spots and drips on the floor had to be mopped up, but the improvement was noteworthy.

"You got ready quickly," Rafe said as he came through the doors to the dining room. He stopped and stared at her. "You look lovely."

That startled a laugh out of her and she touched her damp hair. "Hardly."

One side of his mouth lifted. "Are you hungry?"

She wrinkled her nose. "I'm not sure."

"Come see, then decide." He gestured toward the dining room and held the doors open for her.

The table was formally set along with their good china and flowers. In the center was a plate of sliced fresh melons, sprinkled with a variety of berries not so easy to find this time of year. "You did this?"

He shrugged. "I understand you like your bacon crisp." He lifted two lids. Waffles and bacon and fresh chunky strawberry syrup, exactly the way she liked it. "After you are seated I will bring the whipped cream from the refrigerator."

She stared at him. "How did you manage all this?"

"I am a resourceful man." He pulled out one of the chairs.

"But you—" She pressed her lips together. She didn't want to insult him, but she'd seen the kitchen.

"Sit, please."

She took the chair he offered, and started when he touched her hair. She looked up at him, and he quickly withdrew his hand.

"You must eat before the food gets cold. I did not know how to keep it warm at the table."

"I can't believe you went through all this trouble." She picked up the linen napkin and spread it on her lap. "I don't know what to say."

"Say nothing. Eat." He took her plate and served her a huge waffle and then ladled the slightly steaming strawberry syrup on it.

"Are you trying to tell me I'm too thin?" she asked, staring at the plate.

"No, Brianna." He lightly touched her cheek. "You are perfect."

Her breath caught as she looked up at him. Their gazes held for a moment and her insides fluttered.

His face darkened briefly and then he backed away. "I will get the whipped cream."

With a shaky hand, Bri picked up the glass of orange juice. She sipped it, appreciative of the cool liquid sliding down her throat. Maybe Jessie was right. Maybe Rafe did have a bit of a thing for her. He had his pick of women—that was no secret. And it wasn't as if he was stuck here at the Flying Ace. He could fly to Dallas or Houston or San Antonio at the drop of a hat. Yet he chose to stick around.

And make her breakfast.

She gazed at the beautifully set table. Did he know that red and white carnations were her favorite, or was this a coincidence?

Of course it was a coincidence. But he also knew she liked her bacon crisp. And the strawberry syrup was another favorite of hers...

Darn it! She'd been listening to Jessie too much. This didn't mean he was interested. It meant he was a nice man who wanted to repay his hostess. She sipped the orange juice, waiting for him to return before she started eating. He took an awfully long time just to get whipped cream, but he finally reappeared.

He set the silver dish beside her and then served himself in silence. He sat directly across from her, but she couldn't catch his gaze.

Something was wrong. She felt it in the pit of her stomach. After swallowing the sudden tension in her throat, she forced herself to take a bite. She chewed, swallowed, and still he didn't meet her eyes. "This is wonderful."

He smiled politcly. "I am glad it pleases you."

The food churned in her stomach. He seemed different. Detached. Distracted. Maybe even agitated. "Is anything wrong?"

"Hmm?" He looked up. "No, nothing. I was thinking about this evening."

Her pulse leaped. She'd been thinking about this evening, too. She'd make him dinner...a popular Munir dish Allie had taught her how to make. Or at least had described in detail. Although she'd gotten better, Allie's early attempts at cooking ranked right up there with Rafe's.

Bri smiled to herself. She recognized Rosie's signature strawberry syrup.

"I was thinking about this evening, too," she said finally.

His wary expression made her want to laugh.

"I have a surprise for you." She hoped like heck she could get all the proper ingredients by this afternoon. Allie had a lot of the stuff already stocked in the pantry.

His face became an unreadable mask. "I'm sorry, Brianna. I am flying to Dallas within the hour."

Chapter Nine

He hadn't planned on going to Dallas the other night.
Bri would bet her life's savings on that. He'd made
the last-minute decision to get away from her. The
more she thought about his abrupt departure, the more
convinced she became.

But what had she done to scare him off?

She stared at the neat stacks of paper on her desk.
The inventory was complete. Payroll was finished.
She had already sent the month-end paperwork to
their accountant and Rafe had only been gone for a
day. A day and half, really, but who was counting?

She tidied her desk for the second time, and considered calling Jessie. Her friend had tried to come
over yesterday but Bri had avoided her. She wasn't
sure what Jessie was up to, something about a make-
over she guessed, and Bri certainly wasn't up to
primping for Rafe. The heck with him.

Maybe a trip to the lake would be better. The tran-
quillity of the water and trees always soothed her,
helped her to think straight. Something she'd had
trouble doing all day. Okay, for a day and a half.

When she'd had the distraction of the inventory and payroll, things had gone better. But downtime allowed her to obsess on what she'd done wrong. She just didn't understand it. Rafe had been so warm and solicitous, and then in a blink of an eye he'd become cool and detached.

And for the life of her she couldn't figure out what she'd done wrong. All her childhood she had done everything in her power to keep the peace, to never draw Aunt Elaine's attention.

She'd learned to carry on the tradition in school, and then when she'd come to live with Cord. Life was so much simpler that way. Everybody was happy. Well, sometimes she wasn't, but as long as there was peace, it didn't matter.

The blinds in her office were angled such that the setting sun shined enough in her face to annoy her. She got up to close them, and gazed toward the lake. It would be dark soon but she could get in a swim.

She made up her mind just as the phone rang. After briefly considering letting the machine pick up the message, she grabbed the receiver and greeted the caller.

"Brianna?"

It was Rafe. Her heart lurched. "Yes."

"How are you?"

"Fine. You getting all your business done?"

There was a pause. "Yes."

She bit her lower lip, wanting to ask when he would return. "Your foal is doing great."

"I had no doubt. The Colemans are the best breeders in Texas." He paused again, and then his voice lowered. "Have you thought of a name?"

Not a single one. She'd been too busy working and moping. "Are you serious? You really want me to help choose one?"

"Of course."

"Okay." She sank into her chair and wound the phone cord around her fingers. "Rafe? Why did you call?"

Silence stretched. And then he said, "To see how you were doing."

"Checking up on me for Cord?" she joked, but when he didn't answer right away, her hackles rose. "Are you?"

"Yes, he said you like to have wild parties while he is gone."

Bri's mouth dropped open, and then she laughed. "Yeah, that's me all right." She couldn't stand the suspense another minute. "So," she began casually, "when are you coming home? I mean, back here."

"Ah, perhaps you miss me?"

"No, Hannah Coleman wanted to know."

He laughed softly, as if he knew that was a lie. "I believe my business will be wrapped up sometime tomorrow. At the latest I will return the day after."

Disappointment needled her. "Okay, I'll tell Hannah," she said, and swore she heard him chuckle. "Anything else?"

"You are trying to be rid of me?"

"No, But I want to make a quick trip to the lake before it gets dark."

"The lake? Now?" He muttered something she didn't think was in English.

"Yes, the lake. Why?"

"To swim?"

"It's not dark yet."

"But you are alone. It is not safe."

She laughed. "Now you sound like Cord. It's very safe. I'm a good swimmer and I don't even go in too deep, anyway."

"You know a person can drown in a few inches of water."

"Yes, that's right, but I know this lake and—"

"Brianna, promise me you will not go." The quiet desperation in his voice caught her off guard. "Promise me."

Her heart started to pound. He sounded so concerned. "Rafe, this is silly."

"Promise me, Brianna."

She frowned. If it had sounded like a command, she would have told him to forget it, but he sounded genuinely concerned that she would go swimming alone. "All right," she said slowly. "I'll pass on the swim for today."

"Thank you."

Her stomach flip-flopped. He cared. He had to. "Don't tell Cord I gave in. He's been nagging me not to go alone for a year."

"Can I trust you? You are not simply telling me what I want to hear?"

"You can trust me."

"But can you trust me?"

Bri frowned. "What?"

His brief laugh was wry. "It was a regrettable joke. Sleep well tonight, Brianna."

"You, too."

He didn't say another word. All she heard was the click of the call being severed.

She hung up the phone and then rested her head on the back of the chair. He had to feel something for him to call like that, for nothing, really, and then to make her promise she wouldn't go swimming alone. Maybe if she looked more his type he'd let his interest show. Maybe if she dressed older, wore her hair in a more sophisticated style...

She reached for the phone again. She knew what she had to do and there was no getting around it. She needed Jessie's help.

"MY HAIR LOOKS stupid like that."

"No, it doesn't. It looks very chic and sassy."

Bri sighed, wondering why she had broken down and called Jessie last evening. Desperation, that's why. Now, nearly twenty-four hours later, regret cramped her stomach. "I don't want to look sassy. Just sophisticated."

Jess planted her hands on her hips and glared at her. "Do you want my help or not?"

"I just don't want to look like a cheerleader or prom queen."

"Excuse me, but I was both."

"In high school." Bri patted her hair down. How Jessie had managed to raise it three inches, she had no idea. "That was a long time ago."

"Hey, not that long." Jessie stood back and looked

at Bri with a critical eye. "You could be right. I did get a little crazy with the hair spray. But I like the French twist."

"I don't know…"

Jessie sighed and stuck another pin into Bri's hair. "You're far too young to be so resistant to change. Trust me, you look awesome."

She squinted into the bathroom mirror. "You don't think this is too much makeup?"

"Bri…" Jessie's drawled warning had gotten to be a chorus. "Don't make me call Hannah and Serena over to help gang up on you."

"He's going to notice the difference."

"He'd damn well better. Anyway, like I told you, sometimes you've got to just slap a man upside the head, so to speak."

Bri, stared at the plum eye shadow on her lids, the pink lipstick that, along with a lining pencil, made her lips look enormous. She barely recognized herself. Rafe was going to think she'd gone bonkers.

Or worse, that she'd made herself up for him.

She groaned. Of course, that's exactly what she was doing.

Jessie stopped messing with Bri's hair and stood back. "What's wrong now?"

"I feel stupid."

Jessie's lips curved up in a gentle smile. "You look gorgeous. You should have been a model."

"Right."

"Brianna, honestly, sometimes I could have given that Aunt Elaine of yours a piece of my mind."

Bri stiffened. She hadn't spoken of her aunt often,

and she certainly hadn't bad-mouthed her to Jessie, or anyone else.

"I'm sorry," Jessie said, looking a bit sheepish. "But it irritates me that someone as smart and pretty as you could be so uncertain about herself."

"That isn't Aunt Elaine's fault," Bri murmured, belatedly realizing she hadn't denied the smart and pretty part. "I've always been shy and timid."

"Gee, I wonder why."

"You don't even know her."

Jessie went back to fussing with Bri's hair. "You're right. I shouldn't have said that. I apologize."

Bri stared in the mirror, watching her friend twirl a tendril of hair around her finger and try to make it stay.

Bri didn't know why she'd gotten so defensive. Except Aunt Elaine had taken her in when no one else would. And Bri owed her for that kindness.

"Okay, don't get crazy on me," Jessie said, "but I'm going to slowly pick up the hair-spray can. I promise it won't hurt."

"Oh, no…"

"Close your eyes." Jessie shielded Bri's face with her hand and sprayed the tendril falling down her cheek. "Perfect. But don't touch it."

"No, ma'am." Bri smiled, but she couldn't let go of their earlier conversation. "Why did you say that about my aunt?"

Jessie sighed. "I said I was sorry."

"I'm not being critical, just curious."

"It's nothing specific…I mean, you haven't said

much about her, but I know she raised you rather grudgingly and that she was really strict." Jessie shrugged. "That had to be hard on a kid. And frankly, I think it was the reason you were so shy. Still are, really. It's not easy to live up to a demanding parent."

Bri stared down at her newly manicured nails. "She did the best she could."

"I'm sure she did, and hey, you're here, aren't you? Right where you want to be. That's something." Jessie aimed the hair-spray can at the top of Bri's head.

"Don't you dare."

"You want it to stay put until he gets here."

Bri glanced at her watch. "Oh my God." She pushed to her feet and toddled a moment, unused to high heels. "He's going to be here within an hour. I have to finish dinner and make the sangria."

"Sangria?" Jessie started to collect her makeup. "Planning on getting him drunk?"

Heat climbed Bri's neck and spread through her cheeks. "Yes."

Jessie blinked, clearly startled, and then burst out laughing. "You go, girl."

"I can't believe I said that." Bri kicked off the heels.

"Hey, that's part of the total look. You have to wear those."

"I will. Just not while I'm cooking."

"Need help in the kitchen?"

Bri shook her head and smiled. "Thanks, Jessie." She hugged her friend.

Jessie hugged her back, gingerly. "Don't mess up your hair."

"I won't." She hoped Rafe would do that for her. "Don't forget your curling iron."

"Got it. Okay, I'm outta here. Have fun. And call me first thing in the morning."

As soon as Jessie left, Bri put on an apron and scrambled around the kitchen, checking recipes and timers and her cheat sheet. Almost everything was done. She'd been cooking the lamb slowly, since lunchtime, so that the aroma of exotic spices filled the kitchen. The stuffed grape leaves and couscous needed only to be heated and the saffron rice she would turn on at the last minute.

She went to work on the sangria, tasting and adjusting the sweetness, making it a little more tart than usual. The way Allie liked it. Hopefully she shared the same taste as her brother.

When everything was to her satisfaction, she went to the bathroom to make sure she hadn't done any damage to her makeup and hair. She stared in the mirror in awe. Was that really her? Of course she had seen herself earlier, but with Jessie as a distraction Bri hadn't gotten a full look at herself. She was… somebody else. Certainly not Brianna Taylor. Not the skinny kid from New Hampshire who'd hidden behind textbooks most of her life.

She glared at herself, made a scary face and then smiled widely. The image was her, yet it wasn't. Oh, God, this was so weird. Too weird.

She looked like a tramp. Just like Aunt Elaine had warned.

Bri grabbed some tissues. Maybe if she blotted the lipstick, toned down the eye shadow, got rid of the eyeliner... She brought a tissue to her face but she just couldn't do it. Jessie thought she looked okay. And nothing had changed inside. She was still Brianna. Was it so wrong to want to be noticed by Rafe?

Cord and Allie would be home in less than a week. After that, who knew when she'd see Rafe again? She couldn't let the opportunity to be with him slip past her. They had some kind of chemistry going on. She'd known the moment he'd asked her not to go to the lake alone that he had feelings for her.

It probably meant little to him, but she didn't care. Well, she did, but she was more concerned with not wimping out. Not giving it her best shot. But what exactly was *it*? A night of great sex and then goodbye? Did she want to be a port in his storm when he came to visit Allie or buy more Arabians from the Colemans?

She didn't know, and right now she didn't want to think about it. If she did, she would wimp out. That was her style. Don't do anything daring and don't rock the boat. The heck with it. They were both adults.

She balled up the tissues and threw them in the wastebasket. Tonight she'd be Brianna Taylor, femme fatale. She slipped on the high heels she'd discarded earlier, took a few steps and nearly broke her ankle.

AS SOON AS the Flying Ace came into view, Rafe felt the blood speed through his veins. Anticipation burned in his chest. He had been gone only two days. It seemed like a month—a month that Brianna had plagued his thoughts and his dreams.

The driver pulled the limo in front of the house and unloaded Rafe's bags. When the man started to carry the luggage into the house, Rafe stopped him, gave him a generous tip and sent him away.

Foolish, he knew, but he did not want anyone else present when he saw Brianna. He wanted no distraction for either of them. He wanted the reunion to unfold naturally, to see if she had missed him as much as he had her.

Only two days away and he was behaving like a lovesick schoolboy. Ridiculous. If she were any other woman, he would have bedded her by now. That was the problem. A classic case of wanting what you could not have.

He carried the bags to the front door and was about to ring the bell when the door opened. Brianna stood back to let him inside and it frustrated him that he was unable to see her initial expression.

"Hi," she said finally. "Need help with those?"

He heaved the two heavy bags over the threshold where he left them, and then turned to her. "Hello, Bria—" Thoughts failed him. "Brianna?"

She gave him a shy smile. "Hi" she repeated.

Her hair was up, a few tendrils floating about her flushed face. The light shading across her eyelids made her eyes look so incredibly blue, and her lips, the color of juicy ripe peaches, were like a beacon to his growing hunger for her.

He closed the door behind him, anxious to shut out the rest of the world.

''I hope you're hungry,'' she said, her voice higher than usual. "I made dinner." She fidgeted with her hands. Her nails were painted the same color as her lips.

He wanted to feel them both on his skin...her nails on his back, her lips on his, exploring, taking. He wanted to touch her in return, taste the most intimate parts of her.

She took a step back, dragging her palms down the short black skirt. "If you aren't hungry, it'll probably keep until tomorrow."

The legs she normally kept hidden were long and shapely and threatened his dignity. If he had any sense remaining, he would summon the limo driver to return and take him as far away from Brianna Taylor as possible.

"You look lovely," he said finally, knowing his staring made her nervous. "Stunning."

She cleared her throat. "Thank you." She cleared her throat again. "Jessie was over and we were experimenting with makeup and trying to decide what I should wear to the dance." She shrugged. "You know, girl stuff."

Disappointment sliced through him. This was not for his benefit, but for another man. He smiled. "Your date will be very fortunate."

Hurt flickered in her eyes. "What about dinner?"

He picked up one of the bags. "I am ravenous."

Her lips curved instantly, calling attention to their

lushness, and he questioned the wisdom of sitting across the table from her through the span of a meal.

Agitated, he carried his bag to his room without saying another word or giving her a glance. Perhaps he had returned too soon. He knew she was all right. Her friend Jessica was in town, and the older man, Manny, clearly had his eye out for Brianna.

Rafe dropped his bag on the luggage rack, and then rotated one of his stiff shoulders. Tension cramped his muscles. It would have been more prudent to remain in Dallas until his scheduled meeting. Not come back to fence with temptation.

He unpacked a few things, reluctant to return to her company. That she'd prepared herself for another man should have discouraged him. And perhaps it would have if he was convinced she had no feelings for him. No matter what she said, her eyes did not lie. They reflected Rafe's own hunger, a hunger she was not skilled enough to conceal.

Perhaps he should kiss her. Solve the mystery. Prove to himself that she was like any other woman. A kiss would scarcely breach Cord's trust. A kiss meant nothing—a social greeting embraced around the world. Except that was not the kind of kiss Rafe had in mind.

He wanted to dive into her. Explore her sweetness, taste her innocence. He wanted to lose himself in her softness. He had hoped his absence would give him a better perspective, return him to a world more to his liking, where the women were savvy and willing, and Brianna did not occupy his mind.

But even time and distance could not ease the craving he had for her. In fact, the desire to return had grown from the moment he had arrived in Dallas.

He finished unpacking his toiletries and realized the other bag, the one he had bought in Dallas, he had left in the foyer. No matter, the contents were made up of gifts, something for Aliah, the rest for Brianna. He wondered now if the purchases had been foolish, if Brianna would make too much of the simple gesture.

He laughed to himself. More likely, she would refuse the offerings. She was a woman who expected little. She continually baffled him.

After turning on the shower, he peeled off his clothes, surprised he was anxious to get into his jeans again. Other than his Arabian purchasing trips, he never wore such casual clothes, and certainly not jeans. Even on his initial trip here, he had donned the conventional garb of his people. A lot could be said for tradition. It often gave him comfort in a world that was so swiftly changing.

Once he had showered and felt presentable enough for dinner, he headed for the living room and straight for the bottle of aged scotch. Rafe heard a faint noise coming from the kitchen, from where the familiar aroma of lamb and cardamom wafted out to him like a siren's call.

Had Brianna prepared the special Munir dish for him? He downed a shot of scotch, his mind reeling. She had had to go to some trouble to learn the dish and then gather the proper spices.

Only one way would he find out. He poured another scotch and downed it quickly, knowing the im-

prudence of drinking liquor when he was so sleep
deprived. This was it. No more. He put away the bottle of scotch and went to the kitchen.

He thought he heard voices as he approached. Self-
ishly, he hoped Jessica had not returned. Brianna
liked to listen to the radio. Perhaps that was what he
heard...

Rafe stopped at the door. Brianna was with a man,
the one with whom she had agreed to go to the dance.
She huddled in the corner against a counter, leaning
away from him, pushing the hand away he had on her
hip.

Rafe lost all sense of reason.

Chapter Ten

"Chuck, what on earth has gotten into you?" Bri kept her voice down, not wanting to alert Rafe. What she really wanted to do was scream at the idiot.

He'd come in a minute ago, taking her by surprise. None of the hands came into the house, unless invited, which pretty much didn't happen unless Cord had a holiday party. The guys had their own bunkhouse with everything they needed.

"Chuck, stop it." She swatted his hand away from her face.

"Hold on, darlin', you had a little flour or something on your cheek. That's all."

"I'm not your darling and I didn't invite you to come into the house."

He reared his head back, looking offended. "I heard you yelp and thought you were in trouble. I was tryin' to help out, darlin', that's all."

"I didn't yelp." She moved away from him and turned to the pot on the stove, pretending to stir the lamb. "I burned my finger on the stove and reacted."

"Let Chuck have a look at that finger. I'll kiss it

and make it all better." He picked up her hand but she yanked it away.

"Stop it, Chuck. I mean it."

He looked her up and down, lingering on the exposed part of her thighs just below her hem. "You're lookin' mighty fine tonight, Brianna. Makes my mouth water for next Saturday."

The thought of going to the dance with him made her stomach turn. She made up her mind she wouldn't go. Let him or any of the other hands think what they want about her and Rafe. "You need to leave."

He gave her a cocky smile. "Now, you didn't dress like that not to be noticed."

He moved closer and she backed up. "Hmm, you smell damn good, too."

She found herself in the corner, trapped between him and the counter. He put a hand on her hip and bowed his head, his mouth inches from her throat. "Chuck, get your hand off me, or you can pack up your things and get off the ranch."

He laughed. "You sayin' you'd fire me?"

"Yes."

"Without big brother to tell you what to do?"

"Get out." Her voice shook, not from fear but anger and humiliation. "Right now."

He hesitated, uncertainty in his face. She wouldn't look away but glared back.

"You heard Brianna." Rafe's quiet, deep voice sliced through the air between them.

Chuck took an automatic step back. He turned toward Rafe. "This is between me and Bri here. You got no call to stick your nose in." Brave words but his cocky tone had slipped.

Rafe moved closer. "And she asked you to leave." He smiled. "Now."

Chuck's jaw clenched. He gave Rafe one last resentful glare and then looked at Bri. "I'll talk to you later."

"Only to pick up your final check." She realized she'd been cowering and straightened. "It'll be ready in a week, but you leave today."

His jaw slackened in disbelief. "You're not serious."

Bri went to the phone and dialed the bunkhouse extension. "Hi, Manny, it's Brianna. I need a favor." Her hands shook but she tried not to think about that. She tried not to look at Rafe, either.

"You got it, kid." The familiar sound of the foreman's voice soothed her.

"As of right now, Chuck is no longer with the Flying Ace. Would you and the boys help him load his pickup? I'll explain later."

Chuck let out a vicious curse. "I don't believe this. You're firin' me over a simple misunderstanding?"

"Was that that miserable sidewinder I heard?" Manny asked. "You okay, Bri?"

"Fine. Really. I have to go, but I promise I'll explain later."

"Okay," he said hesitantly, his concern giving her strength. "I'll be waiting for him outside the bunkhouse. Tell him he has two minutes to get his scrawny behind over here or I'm coming for him."

Not that she'd planned on relaying the message, but

before she could, Chuck cursed again and left the kitchen, slamming the door behind him.

"He's on his way, but keep things peaceful, okay, Manny? Promise me."

"Don't you worry none." He hung up, and she replaced the receiver, not looking forward to facing Rafe.

When she finally looked at him, to her utter amazement, he was smiling. She folded her arms across her chest and glared at him. "I can't imagine what you find amusing."

He shook his head. "Pleasantly surprised is more accurate. You did a splendid job."

She rubbed her arms. "I didn't know there was an art to firing someone." She hoped Cord wouldn't be upset. They'd been shorthanded until they'd hired Chuck.

"I believe you know what I mean." He went to the refrigerator and got out a bottle of wine. After uncorking it, he poured her half a glass of Chardonnay. "Here. This will help calm you."

She thought about denying she needed calming down, but that would be pretty silly considering her hands still shook when she accepted the glass. "Thank you."

"You could have called me." He pulled out a kitchen chair for her. "I have so little opportunity to play the knight in shining armor."

She couldn't help but smile. "I didn't know he was going to be a jerk. It all happened so fast."

He took a chair at the table opposite her. "I am truly sorry this happened, Brianna. But you did the right thing. You know, of course, that Cord would have fired the man immediately.'' He grunted. ''After he had given him a good thrashing.''

Would he have fired Chuck? Bri took a small sip of wine. Or would he have assumed it was Bri's fault, that she had led Chuck on with the ridiculous way she was dressed.

No, she was letting old memories play in her head. Aunt Elaine would have taken that attitude. Not Cord. He'd have known Bri had done nothing wrong.

''Brianna?''

She snapped out of her preoccupation to meet Rafe's concerned eyes. ''I hope this hasn't ruined dinner for you.''

''For me?'' His eyebrows rose. ''It is you who has suffered this unfortunate ordeal.''

''I'm okay.''

He reached for her hand and sandwiched it between his large warm palms, chasing away the nervous chill. ''Would you like more wine?''

''No, thanks, I—'' Darn it. She'd forgotten about the sangria. ''I made something to go with dinner. It's a popular drink around here. Sangria. Have you heard of it?''

He shook his head.

''I have my own special recipe.''

He kept hold of her hand when she started to get up. ''I can get it.'' He indicated the refrigerator. ''In there, I assume.''

''There's a glass pitcher.'' She leaned back and let him get the sangria, watching and wondering at the graceful way he did something so mundane as setting the pitcher on the table and getting glasses out of the cabinet.

"Something smells good coming from those pots."

"Oh, right." She stood. "I better get back to the stove."

"Relax." He put a hand on her shoulder, urged her to sit back down and began massaging her tense muscles. "If my nose does not deceive me, I believe that particular dish will be all the more tasty as the spices and flavors meld. Dinner can wait."

She slanted him a look. "You can tell what it is?"

"It is the palace curry, is it not?"

"That's what I intended, anyway." She briefly closed her eyes when he rubbed a particularly sensitive spot, suddenly not caring at all how dinner turned out. "Allie taught me how to make it."

"My sister?"

"Yes." She twisted around and looked up into his disbelieving eyes. "You're going to be surprised at how much she can do around the kitchen."

"Aliah?"

Bri laughed. "Yes, Aliah. She called your chef at the palace and he gave her some of his recipes."

Rafe frowned. "That must have given the entire staff quite a laugh."

"I imagine so."

He looked questioningly at her.

Bri settled back and moved her shoulders a little, hoping he got the hint and started massaging again. "Let's just say Allie was not prepared for life among us commoners."

He laughed, his fingers starting to work their magic

again. "No, I don't suppose she was. However, she seems to have adjusted. In spite of everything, I'm quite proud of her."

"In spite of everything?" She closed her eyes and hung her head to expose more of her nape.

"The fact that I face the guillotine when I return to Munir without her."

Bri's eyes flew open. She sat up straight and turned to look at him.

He smiled. "Ah, you do care."

"That wasn't funny."

"You think we are such barbarians?"

"I don't know what I thought." Embarrassed, she tried to get up, but he laid his gentle but firm hands on her shoulders, preventing her escape.

"How much do you know about Munir?" He started to knead again and she decided it wouldn't hurt to stick around a few more minutes.

"Just what Allie has told me." She exhaled slowly, reveling in his touch. "Have you told your parents about Allie yet?"

"It was my duty."

Bri hesitated. She shouldn't ask since he didn't volunteer... "What happened?"

The pressure of his hands eased a little. "There are some very unhappy members of the family."

"With you or Allie?"

"Neither of us will be smiled upon for a while."

Except Allie would be here, thousands of miles away, safe from anyone's wrath. Rafe would return to face the consequences alone. Yet Bri had heard not one word of complaint or concern for himself. "Is that putting it mildly?"

"You are a very curious young lady."

"How mildly?"

He remained silent for a long moment. Long enough that she turned around to look at him again. His gaze narrowed. "Why do you wish to know this?"

"Because I—because you're Cord's brother-in-law. Of course I care what happens to you." Averting her eyes, she looked down, giving him access to her nape again and gestured for him to continue. "I'm really getting used to this, you know."

He chuckled. "So I see. It has made you most demanding."

Demanding? Her? She smiled. He was partly right. How much she had changed in just one week. That she hadn't hidden in her office or room the entire time was quite a milestone in itself.

And her wayward thoughts! Goodness, she could probably be arrested for some of them. She blushed just thinking about her daydream this morning. The one where she'd crooked her finger at him, and when he came to her, she unbuttoned his shirt and slid her palms up his bare chest.

Of course, that had been a coward's dream, but he was here now, massaging her neck... What would he do if she suddenly got up and kissed him? Would he kiss her back? Tell her to behave? She didn't think he'd do that. She'd seen the heated looks he'd given her. She wasn't that naive.

This was crazy. She didn't need the sangria. His

touch was making her drunk, and a little brazen. At least in her thoughts. She ought to just say the heck with it and listen to Jessie. All Bri had to do was make the tiniest move to let him know she was interested. Men understood even the slightest hint, according to Jessie.

"Why are you tensing again?" Rafe ran his hand up her neck and let his fingers trail her jaw. "I must be losing my touch."

"Ah, I don't think so."

"How about more wine?"

"I want you to try the sangria. You can finish my massage later." She silently cleared her throat. "And that's an order."

He laughed, clearly startled. "I would not dream of disobeying."

She got up and prayed her hands wouldn't shake when she poured them each a glass of sangria. They weren't all that steady, but she did manage not to spill.

He accepted the glass she handed him. "Tell me again the name of this drink."

"Sangria."

"It has alcohol in it, correct?"

"A little." She nearly choked on the lie. Although technically, it was only her version of the fruity wine mixture that had enough to down a horse.

"Are you not having some?"

She smiled and poured herself a small amount. He obviously noticed her mini portion compared to his but said nothing. She waited for him to take his first sip. He seemed hesitant.

Her shoulders sagged in dismay. "What do you think I'm trying to do, poison you?"

His left eyebrow rose. "The thought had not entered my mind, however, now that you have brought up the subject..."

She gasped. "You can't be—"

He smiled and took a sip.

And then did an admirable job of not wincing...too badly.

"You don't like it."

"It's very sweet."

"Maybe I put too much sugar this time." She took a sip, too, although she already knew she'd put a ton of sugar to cover the alcohol taste. Wow! "It is a little sweet. You don't have to drink it if you don't want to."

He shook his head. "I was merely unprepared for the sweetness." He took another small sip. "But there is also a tartness that complements it quite nicely."

She really wanted to kiss him now. He hated the drink, she could tell. But he clearly didn't want to hurt her feelings.

"Why don't we eat now," she said. "I made the lamb spicy just the way you like it. That ought to counterattack the sangria."

His lips curved in a sexy smile that made her insides flutter. "You made the lamb just the way I like it, huh?"

She swallowed and nodded, and then sipped her sangria...a little too noisily.

He took the glass from her, set it alongside his on

the table and then took both her hands. "Did I tell you how absolutely lovely you look tonight?"

She nodded, and then shook her head. Oh, God, she was being a nut, or worse, a child. "Thank you."

He tugged her a little closer. "You smell good."

"It's probably the lamb."

He laughed.

She cringed. *Probably the lamb?* Oh, heaven help her, she wanted to run and hide.

He frowned suddenly, his gaze going toward the back door. "Come." He led her to the window above the sink. "The young man is leaving as you had ordered."

She wrapped an arm around herself. "That's Chuck's pickup."

Outside the bunkhouse, Manny and Joe stood watching him leave. They wouldn't miss him, she knew. He'd had a run-in with both of them at one time or another. Manny had complained he had a cocky mouth, but Cord had talked to Chuck and the tension seemed to disappear.

She thought she ought to go out and thank them, but stopped herself when she remembered what she was wearing. What would they think of an outfit like this? That maybe she'd asked for Chuck's unwelcome attention? Would they wonder what she'd been doing in here with Rafe?

"I am glad to see these men are protective of you."

"A couple of them have worked for Cord forever. Chuck was a new hire."

"Are you all right?"

She realized she was rubbing her arm with a vengeance. "Sure. How about dinner?"

He studied her for a long uncomfortable moment. "Did I not arrive in time?"

"In time?" She started at him, confused. Anger suddenly radiated from him.

"What did this man do to you?"

"Nothing." She adamantly shook her head. "Nothing more than you saw." She sighed dramatically. "You got me relaxed with that massage and now you're getting me all hyped up again."

His eyebrows drew together in a skeptical frown, and then amusement sparked in his eyes. "Are you trying to tell me something?"

"Fishing for compliments?"

He didn't understand the phrase, judging by the puzzled look on his face.

Or else he wanted her to elaborate on what she thought of his magic hands. Right. "It's time for dinner." She turned away before he charmed her into telling all kinds of secrets, and started preparing the food to be heated. "Have another glass of sangria," she said sweetly and bit back a smile at his forlorn expression.

"May I pour you another, as well?"

"Sure." It didn't mean she had to drink it all. If she did she'd get silly. Already she felt some of the effects of the last glass. Maybe she had gotten a tad heavy-handed with the alcohol.

He poured her a full glass, and himself half as much. She kept busy adjusting the gas stove and getting table settings down from the cabinets. She asked him to take the plates and utensils into the dining room, and while he was gone she poured him more sangria.

"Well, everything should be heated and ready in about ten minutes," she said, glancing around the kitchen. "I hope I haven't forgotten anything."

His silence drew her attention. He picked up his glass and frowned at it.

"I'm so glad you like the sangria," she said quickly. "Did I tell you it's my own special recipe?"

He gave her a polite nod, and then took an even politer sip.

She pressed her lips together and turned away. But was swiftly punished for her duplicity when her heel caught and she turned her ankle. Not badly. Just enough to make her whimper.

"Brianna." Immediately he was by her side, his hand at her waist steadying her.

"I'm okay. It's these darn heels. I'm not used to wearing them." She probably shouldn't have admitted that. She straightened. "I'm okay. Really."

His gaze ran down the front of her blouse to her skirt to her heels, and then slowly back up. His eyes darkened, making her pulse race. "It is unfortunate you prepared yourself for that undeserving moron."

She took a deep breath and looked him directly in the eyes. "I didn't do it for him."

Chapter Eleven

Rafe held her gaze. She was clearly nervous and wanted to look away but she met his challenge. Now, what the hell was he going to do about it? He damn well knew what he wanted to do. Kiss her until she begged him to take her to bed. Make love to her until they melted into each other and became one.

What was with this obsession he had with her? How could he rid himself of it? He had tried to stay away. But all his efforts had netted him were a lack of concentration and sleep.

Her gaze was the first to waver. "I'll finish setting the table."

When she turned away he captured her hand. "Brianna?"

Her beautiful blue eyes widened and her lower lip quivered. She stared at him without saying a word.

He lowered his head and her lips parted slightly. She did nothing to resist the kiss as his mouth descended upon hers. Her hands came up to rest lightly on his chest, and he pulled her closer, increasing the pressure of his lips, parting hers with his tongue and exploring the sweetness inside.

Slowly she slid her arms around his neck. Her breasts pressed against his chest, fueling his craving, making him insane with need for her. He ran his hands down her back until he cupped her backside, and pulled her against his arousal. He deepened the kiss and she whimpered.

He slackened his hold of her, and tried to chase the fog from his brain. When he started to retreat, she held his neck tighter. He brushed his lips across hers, touched the corners with the tip of his tongue. That she seemed so inexperienced pleased him. It also alarmed him.

"Brianna." He forced himself back and met her dazed eyes. "I am—"

"Don't say it." She took a big gulp of air. "Don't you dare say you're sorry."

"But I—"

"No." She silenced him with a finger to his lips. "I wanted you to kiss me." The determination in her eyes fueled him with fresh desire. "I want you to kiss me again."

"Brianna, listen—"

She cut him off with a hard kiss on the mouth as she clutched the front of his shirt to hold him captive. He moved his hands to her back again, knowing they were headed for trouble. Perhaps if she felt how aroused he was, if she realized this was not a game, she would back off.

With obvious impatience, she did not wait but pressed her hips against his hardness. She clutched his shirt tighter and sighed against his mouth. The last of his control began to shred and he slanted his mouth over hers, tasting, probing, seeking her honey.

A buzzing sound came from behind them.

They pulled apart but she seemed to have trouble opening her eyes. He realized the sound came from the oven timer. Releasing her, he depressed the button and shut off the noise.

She blinked. "The stove...I have to turn it off."

He did it for her.

A blush climbed her throat and filled her cheeks. "I, um, I guess we'd better eat now. I think the sangria is kind of getting to me."

"Frankly, after the two scotches I already had, I could use some food in my stomach."

Her eyes widened. "Two scotches? Before the sangria?"

He nodded, puzzled by her surprise.

"Oh."

"You believe that to be excessive?"

"No, of course not. I just didn't know." Her gaze went to his mouth and the air started to sizzle again.

"Brianna."

She gave him a wary look and clasped her hands together.

He pulled them apart to sandwich one between his. "I am not sorry I kissed you."

She visibly swallowed, her fingers curling around his hand. "How about some more sangria?"

He smiled. "That would not be prudent." And he truly meant it. He clearly was feeling the effects of the alcohol. Not to lay blame, but he had been foolish to kiss her. Insane to want to do it again. "I will help you take the food to the table."

She nodded, withdrew her hand, looking embarrassed. He almost pulled her back to him, wanting to reassure her. Make her understand that he wanted her more than he had any woman, but he was honor-bound to protect her. But urging her back into his arms would also not be prudent.

They got the meal to the table in silence and then took seats apart from each other. Brianna barely put any food on her plate, but she filled her glass with sangria. She poured him another, as well, and like a fool, he accepted it.

He tasted the lamb first, pleasantly surprised at the spicy blend of the sauce. He looked up to find her watching anxiously.

Her lips turned down at the corners. "You don't like it."

"On the contrary, the palace chef has never made a finer dish."

She wrinkled her nose. "Right."

"And he certainly has never looked so beautiful preparing it."

She laughed softly. "You're incorrigible."

"Perhaps, but I assure you, I do not exaggerate when I tell you this is a fine meal. How did you learn to cook so well?"

She shrugged. "I learned at an early age. My aunt raised me and she worked, so when I came home from school it was up to me to get dinner on the table." Her eyebrows furrowed. "Is the couscous seasoned properly?"

"It is perfect."

She made a skeptical face.

"Why? Do you not like it?"

"I've never had any of this before, but actually, I like it very much." She moistened her lips, the tip of her tongue intriguing him as if it were Munir's legendary hidden treasure. "But I doubt it's perfect."

He had not misled her. The effects of the alcohol had him mellow and yearning…a dangerous combination. The way she touched her hair, drew in her lower lip or widened her eyes slightly tempted him in a way he could not explain. Perhaps he should have another glass of sangria. Better he would get too drowsy to think…to obsess.

"I didn't have time to make dessert," she said, "but it doesn't look as if you're all that hungry, anyway."

Her wounded look got to him. "Forgive me." He took another sip of sangria and then picked up his fork. "My trip tired me and your wine concoction has mellowed me further. But dinner is very much to my liking."

"Good. I made enough for two days." She dabbed her napkin at one corner of her mouth, drawing his rapt attention to her lips.

Now that he had tasted them the craving intensified. He had hoped to have his curiosity satisfied. That one woman's kiss was the same as another, a basic fulfillment of a physical need. He had been so wrong.

Simply recalling her taste, the shy way she responded, the awkward eagerness that followed stirred a lusty longing in him that threatened his very sanity.

"Brianna?"

Her gaze flew to him with a mixture of wariness and anticipation.

"I hope you will understand why I must retire early tonight."

Her expression fell. "Of course."

"I did not sleep well in Dallas."

"You don't need to explain." She picked up her glass and took a large sip, disappointment echoing in the slump of her slim shoulders.

"You are wrong. I very much feel the need to explain why I am such a coward."

"A coward?"

"If I do not keep my distance from you, I am afraid I will not want to be responsible for my actions." He gave a small shrug. "But you see, I am very much responsible, so I must remove temptation."

Her eyebrows drew together in a frown. "Me? I'm a temptation?"

He smiled when her expression went from confused to pleased. "Extraordinarily so."

She touched her hair in that unconscious way he found so sensual. A tangle of blond tendrils floated about her cheeks and she tried to tuck them behind her ear.

"No, leave it," he said before he knew what had happened.

She blinked, and then her startled blue eyes widened, excitement flickering.

"You look beautiful," he whispered.

She took a deep breath. "Thank you."

He had gone mad. Completely and utterly insane.

One moment he told her they could not play with fire, and the next he fanned the flames.

Rafe choked down several more bites of food, unwilling to hurt her feelings, then downed the glass of sangria. He had to put an end to this evening. Tomorrow when he was well rested and the effects of scotch and sangria had dissipated, reason would return. This weakness that governed him would be manageable. Until then he had to keep his distance. Lock himself in his room. Find escape and solace in sleep.

"Brianna, you have prepared a wonderful meal. I have not enjoyed anything as much since leaving Munir." He pushed his plate aside. "Now, I must get some rest."

The disappointment on her face proved him the coward he was when it came to her. He averted his gaze and gathered his utensils. For the first time since university, he was about to clear his own place setting.

Bri wanted to scream. She wanted to cry, too, but neither was an option. She swallowed around the lump of frustrated disappointment in her throat.

What was wrong? She knew he was attracted to her. He hadn't even tried to hide his expression. And goodness knows, there was no concealing what was happening with him south of the border. She got all tingly and warm thinking about his hard length pressing against her tummy.

Any other time it probably would have frightened her, or at least given her a nervous case of hiccups or something. But not with Rafe. The only frightening thing was how much she wanted him. How she would gladly shed her clothes and lie down with him if he only asked. Or made the slightest move.

She stood along with him, picking up as much as she could carry and then followed him into the kitchen. He was going to try to make a quick exit. She wouldn't let him off that easily.

"Do me a favor," she said, annoyed that her voice quivered slightly. "Reach up into those higher cabinets and get down a couple of containers to store this food."

He gave her an odd look, maybe because he knew she was tall enough to reach the cabinets herself, or because he wasn't used to helping around the kitchen. It didn't matter. Detaining him worked. He opened one of the cabinets and stared pensively at the stacks of Tupperware and the recycled empty margarine tubs.

Bri put the dishes in the sink and then started to rinse them, keeping track of him out of her corner of her eye. At the growing look of confusion on his face she bit her lip. How difficult was it to find the proper container?

Finally, he got down several containers, each of them a different shape and size, and then he studied the contents of the ancient cast-iron pot. The leftover stewed lamb wouldn't fit, but he hadn't seemed to realize that yet.

Good. If she kept him busy long enough while she cleaned the kitchen, maybe he'd forget about trying to ditch her.

"All right," he said finally.

She eyed the containers, the cast-iron pot. "All right, what?"

"I have done as you asked."

"Well, would you mind transferring the leftovers?"

He frowned, but began the task.

Bri went back to her own duties, anxious to be done before he got away. While she threw the rinsed plates haphazardly into the dishwasher, a sudden thought occurred to her. She slanted him a suspicious glance.

Maybe it was the sangria that gave her fake courage, but she asked, "Are you trying to avoid me because of Cord?"

Rafe looked at her as if he wasn't sure she was talking to him. "Avoid you? We just had dinner together."

"But you barely got the last bite in your mouth before you started making excuses to leave."

He gave her a dark look and she turned back toward the sink. Darn it! She wouldn't let him intimidate her like that.

"Is it because of Cord?" she asked again.

"Why do you bring up your brother? What does he have to do with us?"

"Nothing. That's exactly my point. But you may think that because he asked you to keep an eye on me or because he's married to your sister, that somehow puts me off-limits."

He raised his eyebrows.

"Off-limits means I'm not—" She waved a hand,

helpless to come up with another term he would understand.

Apparently, comprehension wasn't the problem. He frowned. "Why would my relationship with Cord put you off-limits?"

"It shouldn't. We're both adults. But I get the feeling that my brother has something to do with you—" At a loss for the right word, mortified by what she'd almost said, heat crept up her neck. "Never mind."

Oddly, he let the matter drop. She returned to loading the dishwasher and snuck a peek at him. He almost looked relieved.

As if she had touched on something prickly he wanted to avoid.

Without being asked, he carried the leftovers to the refrigerator and stacked them on the only available tray. Then, to her surprise, he downed the last of the sangria in his glass, and rinsed it out.

She grabbed it from him and hurriedly placed the glass in the dishwasher, closing the door before he got away. "There. That wasn't too bad."

"No, Your Highness, now may I go to my room for the evening?"

At his teasing tone, she spun around to look at him. The quick reaction threw her off balance and she grabbed the counter. But her heel caught in the hook rug in front of the sink and she stumbled, twisting her ankle.

Rafe caught her arm and kept her from falling farther. But it was too late for her ankle. She'd done a number on it. "Ouch! Darn it."

"What is it?" His anxious gaze searched her body.

"It's my ankle. I twisted it."

"Do not move," he ordered, continuing to support her at her elbow while he lowered himself and slipped off her high heel.

He didn't get up right away, but gently probed the tender area with his fingers. His touch was light enough he didn't hurt her.

"Ouch!" Except right there.

He gave her a sympathetic smile. "I believe it is only a sprain."

"Of course. That's all it is. No big deal." She tried to draw her leg away, but he held on.

"However, you cannot put any pressure on it for a while."

She stared down at her feet. One heel on, one heel off. Impossible to avoid pressure, unless he was to carry her to her room...

Her heart pounded. Not a bad plan.

"Well, that's a problem," she said, careful to avoid his eyes. "I have to get to my room."

"Put your arm around my neck."

All innocence, she widened her eyes. "Why?"

"So that I can carry you."

"Oh, no, that isn't necessary." She made a token attempt to stand on the foot, and winced. It really did smart. That was no act.

He gave her a patronizing smile. "Ready to put your arm around my neck?"

She did, smug with the knowledge that he wouldn't be so condescending when she got through with him. The thought gave her pause. She wasn't Jessie or

Hannah, self-assured, spunky, unafraid to risk humiliation and rejection.

At that realization she nearly laughed. She should be a pro at rejection. Why cower now? Still...

She swallowed hard and slid her arm around his neck. She thought he might simply help support her weight, but he actually scooped her up into his arms and cradled her to his chest. The immediate warmth and feeling of security that spread through her body startled her.

It felt as if she had suddenly become invincible, nothing could hurt her. It was the weirdest feeling she'd ever experienced. Complete trust. Yet she hardly knew him.

"I will bring your shoes in to you later." He started toward the hall, his left eyebrow lifting in amusement. "Although you may reconsider the wisdom of such impractical heels."

"It's not the heels. It's me. I'm a klutz."

He held her tighter. "You are as graceful as a swan. I will hear nothing more."

"Yes, Your Highness," she said, mimicking him, but her voice came out breathless instead of teasing.

His gaze met hers, and then lowered to her mouth. She reflexively moistened her lips. His eyes darkened and his nostrils flared slightly.

"Kiss me," she whispered.

"Brianna..."

"Please."

The pulse at his neck visibly pounded. He lowered his mouth slowly, reluctantly, until his lips barely brushed hers. When it seemed as though he was about to retreat, she pushed up and ran her tongue across his lips.

He briefly closed his eyes, and then muttered a curse as he carried her down the hall. "Why must you make this so difficult?"

"I'm not. You are."

He flipped on her light switch in time for her to see annoyance flash in his eyes. She was about to push the envelope when she saw a pair of skimpy panties and a pink lace bra she'd left lying on the bed.

Why she was embarrassed she had no idea. For goodness' sakes, she'd just licked his lips. But to have something so personal lying out for him to see made her face heat up.

Great. A red face...a sure turn-on.

She sighed as he set her down at the edge of the bed. Her skirt rode up to the tops of her thighs and his hungry gaze made her pulse race. Maybe there was hope yet... If she could just keep him from disappearing too fast...

"Is it swollen?"

He stared at her as if she were from Mars.

"My ankle?"

He looked relieved as he hunkered down for an inspection. His hands were large but gentle on her skin. "No, I think you will live."

"Very funny. You're the one who insisted on carrying me in here."

He kept a hand on her calf as he smiled up at her. "By tomorrow you will barely notice."

"It's fine now, really. Although I think I will stay

off it the rest of the night." She stared down at her peach-colored toenails, awfully glad she'd let Jessic talk her into polishing them.

"May I get you anything before I leave?" His gaze wandered around the room, stopping at the impossible-to-miss bra and panties.

"Maybe you could help me turn down these covers?" She pulled the comforter off the pillows but progress stopped at her rear end.

He nodded, and studied the problem. "You will have to lift your—" He gestured to her bottom. "But do not use your ankle."

The truth was, her sprain wasn't that bad, but the pretense kept him in her clutches for a while. She whimpered a little as she pushed herself up and he immediately took hold of her arm for support, and urged her to loop it around his neck while he lifted her.

He rolled the comforter down to the foot of the bed, and then gently let her back down. "What about your nightclothes?" He glanced around, looking oddly nervous. "May I get something for you?"

"No, thanks. I sleep in the nude."

His gaze flew back to her. She was kidding but decided to keep that her secret. His reaction was way too much fun to ruin.

"Well, then I should go."

"Wait."

He shoved his hands into his pockets, his expression wary.

"I have some aspirin in my bathroom, in the medicine cabinet. Would you mind?"

"Of course not. I should have asked." Looking annoyed with himself, he pointed toward the ajar door leading to her private bath. "In there?"

She nodded, belatedly realizing that she had no idea of the condition of the bathroom after her and Jessie's marathon primping.

Too late to worry about it now. He'd already disappeared inside the bathroom. God, she'd just die if she'd left panties hanging on the towel rack. Usually, she was fairly neat, but there had been absolutely nothing usual about today.

Blessedly he hadn't lingered to gawk, because he promptly appeared with the aspirin and a bottle of water she'd left on the vanity. He opened both and she held out her hand.

"Thank you," she said when he dropped two tablets into her palm.

"Anything else?"

She tried to look woeful. "Would you mind sitting with me awhile? Maybe until I get drowsy? It shouldn't be long."

His gaze narrowed.

She pulled the covers up to her chin. "That's okay. I'm being a baby. Chuck is probably in the next county by now."

Rafe's expression darkened. "You believe he would return tonight?"

"No, I'm sure he won't. I'm just being paranoid. Go on to bed."

The abject uncertainty in his face almost made her forgo the charade, tell him to leave her, that she didn't need him, after all. But then his expression became so tender it turned her head and insides into mush.

Unexpectedly, he reached out a hand and she almost ducked away. He touched her hair. "You do not want to sleep like this."

She stared back, unsure what he meant, and then he plucked a bobby pin from her French twist. He removed a second and a third one until her hair tumbled to her shoulders. His eyes never left her face. She held her breath as he withdrew the final pin and plunged his fingers through her hair.

She closed her eyes and arched her neck, exposing her throat. His lips descended, blazing a light trail from her collarbone up to her jaw. When he reached her mouth it was with a controlled kiss, but she clutched the front of his shirt, unleashing his hunger, and his gentle exploration became a fevered conquest.

She tasted the sangria on his lips and wondered how much of this passion had to do with the alcohol with which she'd plied him. Not that she cared. She wanted one night with him. Just one glorious night.

Abruptly, he pulled away. "Brianna, I can't."

"Okay," she said, keeping hold of his shirt, two buttons already unfastened. "Okay. Just stay with me."

She lay back, letting her hands slacken. He seemed to relax some, so she released him and let her eyes drift closed.

The problem was, she wasn't the least bit sleepy. Still, she wouldn't open her eyes, afraid she'd scare him off.

Snuggling deeper under the covers, she inched

more toward the center, giving him room in case he had the sudden impulse to lie beside her. Not that she held much hope, but just maybe he'd feel secure enough with the comforter providing an obstacle.

She shifted a tad to her side so that she could peek at him from under her lashes. His eyes hooded, he looked pretty drowsy himself. She was fairly certain he was feeling the effects of the alcohol and guilt pricked her.

"Rafe?"

His only response was to look sleepily at her.

She withdrew her hand from under the covers and patted the spot on top of the comforter next to her. "I should be asleep soon. Why don't you just lie here? I won't bother you."

A wry smile lifted one side of his mouth as he picked up her hand and returned it to under the comforter. "Sleep."

Deciding it was best not to press, she closed her eyes again. That didn't stop her mind from racing, though. Maybe she'd taken the wrong tactic. Maybe she should have waited until he'd gone to bed and then followed him in.

Oh, God, she doubted she had the nerve to do something that brazen.

A few seconds later, it didn't matter.

When the mattress dipped with the weight of his body.

Chapter Twelve

Bri did the impossible. She lay perfectly quiet and still for an entire hour. Well, okay, it was probably more like ten or fifteen minutes, but it seemed like forever until she heard Rafe's deep steady breathing.

The semidarkness played tricks on her eyes, but once they adjusted she saw that his were closed, his lips relaxed and slightly parted. His jaw had started to get stubbly, which made her smile. He was always so perfectly groomed. She liked this new look a lot. Heck, she liked the old look.

Moving her hand ever so slowly, she lifted it from under the comforter and lightly stroked his face. He stirred, and she froze and started to withdraw. But he captured her hand, drew it back, and kissed the center of her palm.

"Brianna…"

His voice sounded sleepy and she put a finger to his lips and held her breath. When he didn't move, she inched closer until their noses nearly touched. His warm breath, fruity from the sangria, tickled her chin.

Did she dare kiss him? How awake was he? One

way to find out. She snuggled even closer and brushed his lips with hers.

He made a low groaning sound in his throat that startled her, but she didn't back off. She kissed him harder, slipping her hand inside his partially opened shirt and resting her palm on his chest, the coarse hair there surprisingly soft.

He murmured her name again and then parted her lips with his tongue. She opened up to him and he slipped his tongue inside. Eagerly she unfastened two more of his buttons as he continued his leisurely exploration of her mouth.

Finished with his shirt, she unbuttoned hers. Her bra clasp was in the front and she undid that, too. She pushed the cups aside and pressed toward him until she felt his bare skin against her hardening nipples.

The sensation stole her breath away. Dizzy with it, she closed her eyes, and then nearly whimpered when he pushed a strap off her shoulder and palmed her left breast. His kiss, the kneading, all were so sensually slow it was if they were trapped in a dream. He was her prince, and she his willing captive.

Or was it the other way around?

She had plied him with wine, lured him to bed. If he weren't so groggy, would he stay? She didn't want him to leave. She had no idea what would happen tonight, but being this close for now was all she needed.

He retreated from the kiss but his hand continued to knead and stroke. She ached to have his mouth on her breast, but she left him to his own languid pace. If he fell asleep, it would serve her right for giving him so much sangria after his tiring trip. But it didn't matter. He'd spend the night with her. She'd at least have that much.

She stroked her palm down his chest and then let it rest on his belt buckle. His hand stilled. She stiffened, but before she could think, Rafe drew a nipple between his lips, and greedily suckled her breast.

The leisure gentleness was gone from his touch. He wasn't rough or frightening but he went from one breast to the other and then swiftly back again as if he couldn't get enough of her. Then he raised his head and claimed her lips, his hand going straight for her skirt zipper. He yanked it down while kissing her so deeply she couldn't breathe.

"Brianna, I want you so badly," he whispered against her mouth. "I want to make love to you."

In answer, she unfastened his belt buckle with shaky hands. Without hesitation, he shoved off his pants, leaving on only his boxers, his arousal obvious even in the semidarkness. He cast aside her bra and then pulled down her skirt until all she had on were tiny black bikini panties.

Oddly she didn't feel the least bit self-conscious under his gaze. How could she when he looked as though he wanted to devour her? It was a thrilling sensation, and when he cupped her breasts and then ran his palms over her skin down to her thighs, she thought she just might die with the pleasure of his touch.

"Brianna, I need to be inside you," he whispered hoarsely as he bowed his head for a kiss.

She expected him to be a little rough. He was achingly gentle. "Yes," she said softly. "Yes."

He slipped his hand inside her panties and then drew them down her thighs until she was totally naked. She dipped her fingers into the elastic of his boxers, feeling a little shy suddenly. Thankfully, he didn't seem to notice but simply rid himself of the boxers.

Bri tried not to stare. He was hard and thick, and truly magnificent. Her pulse sped out of control, and she resisted the impulse to squeeze her thighs together.

When he slid a finger inside her, she did tense. But he went slow and easy and she thrust toward him, ignoring the slight sting when he met her barrier. He moaned and lowered his body over hers, and then filled her with more pleasure than she'd ever known.

RAFE DESPERATELY NEEDED water. His mouth was drier than the Sahara Desert. His head was in no better shape. It pounded and he had not even opened his eyes to the light yet. Something he was in no hurry to do.

In spite of his discomfort, he had had the most incredible dreams. Sensual dreams. Erotic dreams. All of them about Brianna. Even now he could smell her scent. Innocent yet mysterious. Seductive. Maddening.

He breathed it all in, and swore he could feel the silk of her hair. Her skin. He refused to open his eyes. He did not want to fully awaken. Not yet. Not when the sensations were so real. Too intoxicating.

He reached behind his head to adjust the pillow and

felt a slight weight on his chest. And then a movement. His eyes flew open.

A tangle of silky blond hair lay in a cloud under his chin.

He blinked.

Brianna lay beside him, her fist curled into a ball and resting on his exposed chest. Her back was bare to the sheets that pooled at her waist.

What the hell—

Memories of last night rushed at him. Memories, not dreams. They had made love. He had broken the vow he had made to himself. Angry and panicked, he started to slide out of bed when he heard the knock at the door. He glanced around the peach floral room.

Brianna's room.

What the hell had he done?

Another knock.

"Bri? Are you there?"

She stirred, moaning softly, opening her hand and spreading it on his chest.

Numb, Rafe stared at the door. Was that Cord's voice? How could it be?

Another knock. "Brianna?"

The knob turned just as Rafe gathered enough wits about him to sit up. Brianna murmured something and fell back into the pillows, her breasts bare.

He pulled the sheet over her just as the door opened.

"Brianna, I'm sorry I didn't want to startle—" Cord ducked his head in and stared at Rafe. His gaze fell to Brianna, who started to wake up.

She murmured something and rubbed her eyes.

Cord's furious gaze met Rafe's. "What in the hell is going on here?"

At his raised voice, Brianna's eyes opened. She blinked, still dazed with sleep, and then looked at her brother as she got up on one elbow. The sheet slipped and Rafe grabbed it before she gave everyone a show.

"What's wrong?" Aliah came up behind Cord and craned her neck for a look. Her eyes widened on Rafe, and then her gaze bounced to Brianna. "Rafe!"

Brianna yawned. "What are you doing home, Cord?"

He took a determined step into the room but Aliah clutched his arm. "Come on. Let them get dressed."

Rafe was too stunned to speak. Stunned and ashamed. He could barely remember a thing after sitting at the edge of her bed last night.

"Cord, please." Aliah held on to his arm. His eyes blazed with fury.

Brianna apparently started to realize what was happening and scrambled to a sitting position, clutching the sheet to her breasts. "Oh my God."

Cord tried to take another step but Aliah pulled him back.

"Cord Brannigan, you are coming with me right now." She gave him a hard tug, and the fury in his expression slackened.

"We will talk, Cord," Rafe finally said. "But please give us a moment."

"You're damn right we'll talk."

"Yes, honey, you will," Aliah said in a soothing voice and managed to drag him out of the room. She shot a parting glance at Rafe, a mixture of disbelief and accusation.

As soon as the door closed, Brianna fell back into the pillows and covered her face with her hands. "Oh my God."

The sheet slipped and exposed one rosy pink nipple. Rafe quickly averted his gaze. For a moment. And then he helplessly turned back to look at her. She was perfection. Utter perfection.

Angry with himself, he briefly closed his eyes and muttered a curse. Beneath the covers he was naked and half-aroused.

And Brianna? Was she totally naked?

The temptation to check was strong. Too strong. He half rolled, half fell out of bed, and then struggled to keep his balance after his feet hit the carpet. His boxers were on the floor and he pulled them on.

She peeked at him from between her fingers. "Oh, Rafe..." Her eyes got glassy as if she was going to cry and his gut clenched painfully. "I'm so sorry."

"You?" He stared, confused. "I am in your room. I took advantage of you. I—" He took in a deep breath when his gaze fell to her partially exposed breasts. He wanted her again. In spite of everything, he wanted to sink himself inside her...

Another memory assaulted him. She had been a virgin... He cursed viciously to himself and looked around for his pants and shirt. His trousers were heaped on the dresser and his shirt draped over the nightstand near Brianna.

"You don't understand." She shook her head, her

eyes oddly pleading, her knuckles pale from clutching the sheet to her breasts. "It wasn't you."

For possibly the first time in his life, Rafe did not know what to do or say. Shame paralyzed him. What had he done? He had dishonored Brianna, himself, Cord and Aliah. How could he ever look himself in the mirror again?

He jerked on his shirt and hastily fastened the buttons. How the devil could he have let down his guard and do something like this? He cleared his throat. "Brianna…"

"No, stop it. Just hear me out and then—" She started to leave the bed and then obviously realized she was naked. Her gaze flew around the room. "Where's my blouse?"

He spotted it tangled with the sheets and retrieved it. "And your skirt?"

"I know where it is. Would you turn around, please?"

He did as she asked, perplexed by her civil behavior. Why was she not lashing out at him? Flinging accusations? He stared at the wall while she dressed. No, of course she would not. She had made her desire for his attention clear. Even though she did not fully understand what she had asked.

Nevertheless, she would not throw him to the lions now. She would accept responsibility, as misplaced as it would be.

It was up to him to not allow such a travesty.

"You can turn around now," she said softly.

She stood near the bed, her feet bare, her arms

crossed protectively over her chest. She gave him a tiny smile.

"Brianna, I—" He gestured helplessly. "I find I am at a loss for words.

"I can explain."

He shook his head. "This is not your responsibility to claim. I knew better. It was my own weakness that...I only wish that—"

"That it never happened?" She looked wounded. "I don't, but then again I was the one who lured you in here."

"You lured me?" Rafe started to laugh.

"Brianna?" Cord's loud voice and angry knock startled them both. "Bri, I want you to come out here."

She drew in her lower lip, but not before Rafe saw how it quivered. "In a minute."

"Stay." Rafe lifted his hand to touch her arm, but quickly lowered it. "I will speak to him."

"No. Absolutely not. I will give him the courtesy of an explanation, but he's my brother not my father." She lifted her chin, tugged down the hem of her skirt. "I am an adult and this is my house, too."

The look of uncertainty on her face dealt him another hand of guilt. He forced a smile and held out his hand. "Come. He has been patient long enough."

"Brianna." Cord's voice briefly drew her anxious gaze toward the door.

She ignored Rafe's hand and grasped the doorknob. "You don't have to talk to him."

"I know."

"In fact, let me do the talking." She hiccuped, and

then turned the knob. "You don't know the whole story."

"What story?"

Too late.

The door opened. Cord's angry glare met Rafe's eyes.

"Come on. Let us all go into the living room and have some hot tea." Aliah pulled at Cord's sleeve until he finally gave in and followed her down the hall. But not without tossing a few more murderous glares over his shoulder.

"Ignore him," Brianna whispered as she and Rafe trailed them to the living room.

"Right."

"And remember, I'll do the talking."

Rafe smiled, in spite of himself. She had spirit. Beauty. Intelligence. Grace. And she was innocent. Or had been. The smile disappeared. What the hell had he done?

She took a seat directly across from her brother and unflinchingly met his eyes. "What are you doing home early?"

"A hurricane is approaching the western Caribbean." Aliah darted a look at Rafe. "You should have heard about it. Hurricane Tina has become national news."

Rafe gritted his teeth. Her expression and tone implied that perhaps he and Brianna had been too occupied to watch the news. "I was in Dallas until last night. On business. I was there for two days."

Cord snorted. "I'd question why you left Brianna

alone like that, but obviously she was better off without you.''

"Left me alone'?'' Brianna glowered at her brother. "So he *was* supposed to be my baby-sitter.''

Cord let out an exasperated sigh. "Come on, Bri, don't try and change the subject. Anyway, you know it wasn't like that.''

Aliah muttered a curse in their language that would have shocked Rafe at any other time. "Cord, what is going on?''

He gave her a sheepish look. "Nothing.''

She continued to glare at him. Both women waited silently for his answer.

"Come on, Allie. You don't think I should worry about my sister?''

Her eyebrows arched. "Worrying and interfering are two very different matters.''

"Thank you, Allie,'' Brianna said, and sent Rafe a withering look. "So he was only teasing, right?''

If she were just angry, he would not care so much, but she was hurt, as well. He read it in her body language and saw the pain shadowed in her eyes. Did she think the attention he paid her stemmed solely from her brother's request? Or was this about last night's betrayal?

Guilt and shame claimed Rafe once more.

He took a deep breath and forced himself to hold Brianna's gaze. "I stayed here to await the birth of the foal, as I have explained. Cord merely mentioned he was glad Brianna would have company.''

Cord grunted something unintelligible. "Look, you're all missing the point, and I think you two ladies ought to go to the kitchen and have coffee while Rafe and I get to it.''

Aliah's eyes narrowed. She folded her arms across her chest and settled back in the sofa, clearly planning to go nowhere. Brianna remained maddeningly silent, her expression haunted.

Cord took a stab at stubborn silence for a moment and then asked, ''What the hell were you thinking?''

Rafe had never felt so powerless in his life. ''I have no excuse.'' He looked at Brianna, her face pale, her fists clenched in her lap. ''Your sister is beautiful and generous of spirit, a very remarkable young woman in many ways, and I—'' His chest tightened as their gazes locked. ''And as I have already said, I have no excuse.''

No one said anything for a long tense moment. Rafe wished everyone but Brianna would disappear. He had the most insistent urge to pull her into his arms, let the consequences be damned. But it would not be fair to Cord.

Only two weeks earlier, had Rafe not been in the same situation? Placed in a position to defend his sister's honor. He had been far more furious and intolerant than Cord was being now, and yet Rafe knew Cord loved Aliah. While Rafe only…

His throat grew dry as he continued to stare at Brianna. What did he feel for her? Affection, certainly…a great deal, in fact. And a protectiveness he did not quite understand. He did not miss that irony. He was undoubtedly physically attracted to her… more than any other woman in his memory. But what did these feelings mean?

Cord loudly cleared his throat and Rafe finally dragged his gaze away from Brianna. Aliah watched him with a curious expression, while Cord glanced speculatively at his sister.

When he returned his attention to Rafe, Cord seemed remarkably less angry. "I know what I saw," he finally said. "There's not much use in revisiting the incident. I guess my question is, what are your intentions?"

Brianna started to comment but sputtered in her haste. She held up a hand. "His intentions? What about mine?"

Aliah laughed, and then immediately sobered when her husband glared at her.

"Now, Bri, this is between Rafe and me."

Brianna gasped. "I can't believe you said that."

"Dammit." Cord wearily rubbed his jaw. "You know what I mean."

"No, I don't." Brianna stood and calmly adjusted her skirt hem. Her hands shook slightly. "More important, I don't care."

"Bri, where are you going?"

She ignored Cord, and Rafe knew better than to try to get her to listen, but when Aliah called out to her, she stopped.

"May I say something before you leave?" Aliah asked.

Brianna nodded slowly but she stayed where she was.

Aliah cast a nervous glance at her husband. "In our country we have a custom." She looked at Rafe. "Right?"

Fear drenched him like a torrential downpour. The last time she had spoken those words, the situation had ended in disaster. "This is America, Aliah. We both know customs here are different."

She shook her head. "It doesn't matter. You are the heir to the throne. Munir needs your leadership. But you must do what our people expect of you to keep their trust and confidence."

Tempted to communicate with her in the privacy of their own tongue, he resisted such rudeness and with a pointed look he said, "I believe we have had a similar conversation not long ago. To which I might add, has come a most disagreeable conclusion."

Her eyebrows rose in indignation. "I beg to differ."

Cord grunted with impatience. "What are you two talking about?"

Brianna sighed. "They're talking about how Allie tricked Rafe into leaving her here in Texas."

"And as we can all see," Aliah said, reaching for her husband's hand, "the situation has ended quite well."

"You deliberately mistake my meaning." Rafe gave his sister a warning look, which she blithely ignored with a lift of her chin. "I admit that at first I merely accepted your marriage, but I have seen how truly happy you are and my approval is uncensored."

"This is all really terrific," Cord said with undisguised sarcasm. "But what the hell does any of this have to do with Bri?"

"Good question." Brianna continued to stand near the door, arms crossed defensively.

Rafe looked back to his sister and captured her gaze. "Nothing."

Aliah's lips curved in the barest of smiles before she turned her attention to Brianna. "According to Munir custom, because you have been publicly discovered, my brother must offer you the sanctity of marriage."

Chapter Thirteen

Marriage?

To Rafe?

Bri's crazy heart thudded. Even as her body reacted, her mind held on to reason. There would be no marriage. He wouldn't ask, and she wouldn't accept even if he was foolish enough to succumb to such an antiquated tradition.

"Allie, you're really something," Bri said, doing everything in her power to keep her voice steady, and her gaze off Rafe. "This is not the Dark Ages. Last night was no big deal."

"No big deal?" Allie's eyes widened. "I know you better than that, Brianna Taylor. And I know my brother better than that, as well."

"Enough, Aliah." Rafe abruptly stood. "Cord, I would like to speak with you alone."

Cord nodded solemnly.

Bri took a step back into the room. "Why?"

"I thought you were leaving,"

She glared at her brother. At least she wasn't shaking anymore. She was too angry. "If you and Rafe are planning on discussing me, don't waste your time."

"Brianna, please, give us just a moment." Rafe gave her that smile that normally made her knees weak. Not now. Not when he was being so darn patronizing.

Besides, he and Cord seemed to have all the answers. They arrogantly thought they knew what was best for her. The hell with them. "Tell you what," she said finally. "You two can discuss me, or whatever you feel the need to discuss, all you want." She waved a hand. "Take the rest of the day. I don't care. Just keep me out of any of your well-intentioned but misguided solutions."

"Brianna, wait." Allie got up from the couch and hurried after her.

Bri headed down the hall back to the privacy of her room. She didn't mind talking to her sister-in-law, in fact she kind of wanted to explain last night, but she wasn't about to wait around any longer and have to look at those two macho idiots. Allie would catch up.

By the time Bri got to her room she was out of breath. Not because she was out of shape, but God only knew when the last time she'd exhaled. Her stomach was in knots and her head pounded like the devil.

Part of the problem was the sangria. She'd had more than usual last night, and she really hadn't eaten much all yesterday. Which showed exactly how smart she was. She idly wondered if she could get away with a loud scream. Just one. The release would make her feel tons better.

She sat at the edge of her bed and then threw herself back flat on the mattress. Rafe's scent still clung to the sheets, and she held her breath again.

"Brianna?" Allie stood at the open door.

Bri sighed. "Come on in. Close the door."

Allie had already started to shut it. "I'm not too happy with them, either." She stretched out on the bed beside Bri, lying on her side, using her hand to support her head as she stared with open curiosity. "We should have called before coming home."

Bri closed her eyes and groaned. "I should have locked my door."

Allie laughed softly. "That was not what I expected you to say."

"What?" Bri opened one eye.

"Never mind." Allie straightened her arm and let her head rest on it. "Are you in love with my brother?"

"Love? Of course not. Why would you ask such a thing?"

Allie's lips curved in a mischievous smile.

"Because of last night?" Bri tried to sound blasé and ended up sounding miserable.

"Will you not admit your feelings because he is my brother?"

"There's nothing to admit." Bri stared at the ceiling, inwardly cringing at what she was about to say. "A little recreational sex doesn't necessarily mean we were in love."

"True." Allie paused. "Except for the way you look at each other."

Bri opened her mouth in disbelief. "We do not look at each other. I mean, not in any special way."

"I know my brother." She lifted her chin in a smug angle. "I know when he is interested in a woman."

"So?"

"He is more than interested in you."

Bri's entire nervous system nearly shorted out. "He is not."

"I believe I am a better judge than you in this instance."

Bri disliked her superior tone. "Really?"

Allie grinned. "You are far too smitten yourself to be a good judge of anything."

She made a dismissive sound but her heart beat faster than native war drums. "You're a romantic, Allie. And you're delusional."

"What does that mean?"

Bri smiled wryly at her sister-in-law's regal tone— one that not only expected obedience, but demanded an answer that met her satisfaction. It reminded Bri how different from each other they were, and not just in temperament. Allie possessed a confidence that had been inbred, something that inspired childish envy in Bri.

"It means that you're crazy," she said, and smiled when Allie looked affronted. "In a nice sort of way, of course."

"Crazy is never nice. However, I understand why you want to change the subject, but I simply won't let you."

Bri issued a heartfelt sigh. "There's no subject to change or discuss or anything else." She paused pensively, knowing that claim would hardly put the matter to rest. "Yes, I think your brother is attractive. And I like him a lot. But I'm not stupid. I know there can't be anything between us."

"Why?"

"Allie…" Bri sat up in disgust. This conversation was going nowhere. Except to upset her. "I think I'll go for a swim."

"Why would you not consider my brother a suitable match?"

That startled a laugh out of Bri. "Are you kidding? It's the other way around."

Allie frowned. "You think you would not make a good wife for him? Why?"

"Oh, Allie, wake up." Bri turned to her dresser when she felt the silly prick of tears. She'd been such a fool to harbor the slightest hope, but everyone didn't need to know that.

"Tell me." Allie's quiet voice was right beside her.

Bri looked down at the hand her friend had placed on her arm. "I'm not the right—" Oh, God, the last thing she wanted was to sound pathetic. "We're both very different. You know that."

"Cord and I are different."

Bri thought a moment. "Not really."

Allie's eyebrows rose in amusement. "No?"

"Well, in some ways, of course, since you come from different cultures. But in every way that counts you're very compatible. You share the same value system and moral ground and—'' Allie's big grin stopped Bri. "What?''

"Nothing. Go on. This is fascinating.''

Bri blinked, and did a quick mental replay of their conversation.

Allie laughed. "Thank you for proving my point. You and Rafe are a lot more alike than you think.'' She gave Bri a playful nudge. "In all the ways that count.''

Annoyed, Bri concentrated on rooting through her drawer. Allie didn't get it. And Bri wasn't up to explaining how vastly different she was from her own brother, how they had grown up in totally dissimilar environments, that the difference in their social skills alone stretched a country mile wide.

Cord at least knew how to act and say the right things in almost any social circle. All Bri could do with any consistency was blush and get tongue-tied.

She plowed through a stack of shorts she hadn't worn for two seasons and another pile of old T-shirts. Where the heck was her swimsuit, anyway? If she didn't find the darn thing within the next five seconds, she'd go to the lake without it.

"Brianna, I wish you would talk to me.'' Allie's dark eyes were serious, almost pleading. "We are sisters now, right?''

Bri smiled and nodded.

"Then we must confide in each other. Trust each other.''

Bri shrugged. "I've never had a sister,'' she said unnecessarily.

"Neither have I.'' Allie's wistful expression

touched Bri. "I have two cousins but they lived too far from the palace for me to see very often."

"What about friends?"

Allie's eyes widened in surprise. "I had a tutor and a nanny. The only other children around belonged to the palace staff, but they were not allowed to play with me." A mischievous smile touched her lips. "Although I did have one friend who used to sneak into my study chambers to play with me. Until her mother, the second-floor maid, caught her and sent her away."

Bri's heart squeezed. She'd never considered how lonely life had been for Allie. A good lesson that money and privilege wasn't everything. "And Rafe?" she asked slowly. "How was his childhood?"

"Ah." Allie's smile turned wry. "A boy is held to different standards. He definitely had more freedom. More friends." Allie shrugged. "More everything."

Bri stared down at the mess she'd made in the drawer, unsure if this conversation made her feel better or worse. She certainly was feeling more humble, that was for sure. How shortsighted she'd been, and too wrapped up in memories of her own unhappy childhood.

"But in many ways, Rafe has had a more difficult time. So much is expected of him. Both personally and politically. Too much, in my opinion." Allie squeezed her arm. "He is a good man. He will do what's right."

Bri had started to mellow, but that effectively broke the spell. "What makes you think I'd want to marry your brother?"

"Because he is handsome, kind, generous and rich."

"And he'll do what's right."

Allie reared her head back. "Is that so wrong?"

Bri abandoned her search and sank to the edge of the bed. She was so darn tired all of a sudden, she wanted to curl up under the covers. "Why did you marry Cord?"

Allie blinked. "What an odd question. I love him, of course."

"So you must understand that I want to marry for love, too."

Allie smiled and sat beside her. "Are you telling me that you have no feelings for Rafe?"

"No," Bri said slowly, cautiously. "Obviously I do or I wouldn't have been in bed with him." Heat rose swiftly to her cheeks. "But love has to go both ways." Bri shook her head. "I know Rafe likes me, and there's a certain physical attraction between..."

Allie burst out laughing.

"Mind sharing the joke?"

"Yes, you could say a certain physical attraction." Allie laughed again. "Enough for sparks to light up the night like fireflies."

"You've been home all of one hour and you've formed this opinion?"

"As I have already said, I know my brother. I saw how he watched you the days before Cord and I married." She sighed, looking forlorn suddenly. "It may be my fault we arrived home without Cord calling first. I mentioned my observations to him, and he was not as happy as I was over the match."

"There is no match, Allie. Don't you get it?"

"There could be if you weren't so stubborn."

Bri had enough. No more soft-stepping. "Okay, you look me in the eyes and tell me that Rafe could marry a westerner without any repercussions."

Allie blinked. "Rafe is free to marry anyone he wishes."

"Is he?"

Allie looked away. "Of course."

"Allie?"

"They expect too much of him. My father, my uncles, our people." Allie threw up her hands.

Bri smiled at Allie's defense of her brother. It had always been obvious how much she adored and respected him. That she even thought for a minute that Bri was good enough was really something.

"That isn't the point." She squeezed Allie's hand. "Or on second thought, maybe it is. If Rafe is already getting a lot of pressure, he certainly doesn't need additional problems brought on by an unsuitable wife."

The spark of awareness and then quiet resignation in the other woman's eyes made Bri's heart drop. Why she was reacting with such melancholy she didn't know. What she'd said was the absolute truth. Nothing new or profound. She would be a liability to Rafe. Plain and simple.

Oh, God. Bri's chest tightened painfully. There was nothing plain and simple about it. She didn't want to be a liability to him. She wanted to…

She wanted…

She abruptly stood before she did something stupid

like start crying in front of Allie. All of this seductive talk of marriage and the attraction Allie noticed had gotten Bri all sappy and needy. Even hopeful.

Dammit. She knew better.

"Where are you going?" Allie jumped up, but Bri had already made it to the door.

She hated leaving without an explanation. Allie didn't deserve that, but Bri couldn't trust herself to speak. Anyway, better everyone had a chance to cool off and time to think rationally.

She heard Cord's and Rafe's voices coming from the living room and she was tempted to stop and listen. But she knew Allie would show up and blow the whistle anyway, so Bri hurried to the kitchen and then let the back door close softly behind her.

RAFE HAD STOPPED listening to Cord five minutes ago. His head alternated from pounding from too much sangria and spinning with the knowledge of what he had done last night. He should be talking to Brianna right now, not Cord.

What was she thinking? She was embarrassed, that was certain. He hoped Aliah provided comfort to her in some way.

Hell, she was probably suggesting styles of wedding gowns.

Oddly, the idea did not put him too ill at ease.

Cord growled his name. "Are you listening to me?"

"Not at all." Rafe stood, and realized that his shirt was not buttoned properly.

Cord frowned. "Well, that was honest. Where are you going?"

"I need to talk with Brianna."

"Yeah, right. Like you did last night?"

Rafe breathed deeply. He understood a brother's anger, he reminded himself, before he told Cord to shut the hell up. "Would you rather I ignore her? Offer no apology or comfort? Is that what she would want?"

"No, but I would." A faint, grudging smile lifted the corners of Cord's mouth. "Dammit, Rafe, it's not that I have anything against you personally."

"I understand."

"You don't. Brianna and I...well, our relationship is still pretty new and it took her a long time to get that she belongs here as much as I do. She doesn't talk about her past much, but I do know she didn't get much emotional support. She's just beginning to come out of her shell, but she's still real fragile."

Rafe nodded, the word *fragile* echoing in his mind. "I am not sure yet what I will say to her."

"Just don't make promises you can't keep."

In spite of Aliah's earlier declaration, surely no one expected him to propose marriage to Brianna. Although he could not find a better wife, not in temperament or beauty.

He shoved the dangerous thought from his mind. His family would not readily accept her. Life in Munir away from her newfound family would be strange and lonely. The oil business and diplomacy demanded much of his time. He traveled often, sometimes for a month at a time.

Fragile.

The word bounced relentlessly inside his head

He recalled a butterfly he had caught as a small child. He had tried to capture its golden beauty inside a jar. It lived only a matter of hours. Guilt had haunted his dreams for weeks.

He could not do that to Brianna. She belonged here, where she had friends and family and everyone loved her, where she felt needed with her work.

Perhaps he could not find a better wife, but she could certainly find a far more suitable husband.

Chapter Fourteen

Last night had been so utterly perfect, how could this be happening? How could she feel so horrid inside? It wasn't right. Bri broke through the trees shadowing the lake.

The mere sight of it immediately calmed her. Glassy sparkling water reflected the blue of the sky and the tall emerald pines along the north shore. She'd claimed this tiny piece of the Texas hill country as her own as soon as she'd seen it the third day after she arrived. No one else came here. The locals seemed to take the small oasis for granted.

She sank to the grass where it thinned out to meet the rim of the lake, unconcerned about the way her skirt rode up her thighs. In truth, there were many places as calm and beautiful surrounding Bridle. But this one was all hers, a sanctuary, a balm to her wounded spirit. Nothing could touch her here. She was free of worry and regrets. Even if only for a few hours.

"Brianna?"

Startled by a dark voice that set her heart pounding,

she twisted around. "Rafe? What are you doing here?"

"We need to talk."

"You followed me?"

He shook his head. "I knew you would be here."

"How?"

His mouth curved in a wry smile. "Perhaps you thought I was not listening."

She remembered their conversation a week ago when he'd asked about the lake. God, had it really only been a week? "If you were truly listening, you would have understood I don't like company when I'm here."

He lowered himself beside her. Close enough that their thighs nearly touched.

She yanked down the hem of her skirt. Not that it helped much. The skirt was far too short. She never dressed this way. What must they all think?

Bri slid a glance his way and realized he had changed his clothes. Probably even had a shower. Yup, his hair was damp. Great. She couldn't imagine what she looked like right now. She'd been in too big a hurry to get away to think about cleaning up.

She sighed.

He touched her arm. "Your brother worries about you. That is what brothers do. Do not be self-conscious."

"I know." She sighed again. "Why did they have to come home so early, anyway?"

"Fate."

She frowned at his somber tone. "I don't understand."

He briefly closed his eyes and then turned his head to look out over the water. He didn't speak for several long minutes. "I tried to stay away. I failed you. I failed Cord."

"So you think fate stepped in to save the day?"

Annoyance wrinkled his forehead.

Tough. She was annoyed, too. And her head still pounded. *And* she needed a shower.

"I am surprised you look upon this situation as a joke."

"I'm surprised you consider it fate. I figure that makes us even."

He studied her for a moment and then gave her a faint smile. "Cord thinks you are only now beginning to come out of your shell."

Amazingly, she didn't blush. Two weeks ago she would have apologized for sounding too assertive. "It seems you both assume too much about me."

"Perhaps." The amusement left his face and he again turned toward the lake. "And perhaps you assume too much about me."

She didn't know what he meant, but she didn't dare ask. She followed his lead and stared out at the water, tracking the reflection of a crow flying overhead. Heck, she didn't know what was worse—to set herself up for an answer she wouldn't like, or not knowing what he was thinking.

"What were Cord and Allie doing when you left?" she asked, wanting to break the silence.

"Cord went to the bunkhouse to let the foreman know he was back, and Aliah started breakfast." One side of his mouth lifted, and Bri smiled, knowing exactly what he was thinking.

"She cooks pretty well now. You'd be surprised."

"If, as you said, she instructed you on last night's dinner, I am already impressed." His gaze found Bri and there was no mistaking the fondness in his eyes.

But of course she already knew he liked her. But he liked Hannah and Jessica, too. And then she remembered the way he had kissed her last night, the way he'd slid inside her and moaned her name. Goose bumps marched down her arms.

"So why did you come here?" She couldn't believe she had the nerve to lead him on. "I don't see that there's anything more to say."

His gaze narrowed slightly. "I do not believe you."

"You think I'm lying?"

"I think you are being evasive."

She looked out at the lake again. It was too hard being this close and to look him in the eyes and not spill her feelings for him. She had to steel herself, be prepared for the token offer of marriage. Even though she didn't think it would really come, that didn't stop her adrenaline from climbing at the thought.

On the other hand, since the offer would be only a token, maybe...

"What are you thinking?"

She started at the huskiness in his voice. "Private thoughts."

He laughed. "Touché."

"If you want to say anything about last night, I

wish you'd get it over with.'' She wouldn't look at him but felt the intensity of his stare.

"I will not insult you by apologizing again.''

"Good.'' She picked up a pebble and skimmed it across the water. "And I won't remind you that I was the one who seduced you.''

"Brianna—'' He stopped. Shook his head. "Fair enough.'' He paused. "I have one question for you to consider.''

She nodded, her pulse picking up speed, so that the next pebble she tried to skim sunk dismally below the surface.

"What would be your most ardent wish for tomorrow?''

She turned to stare at him. "What?''

"After last night,'' he said, his gaze unwavering, "what would you wish for the future?''

"Between us?''

He slowly nodded.

"I wish everything could go back to normal. Like it was before. Like nothing happened.''

His eyebrows rose. "Like nothing happened.''

"You know what I mean.'' She wanted to take it all back and start over. Her answer had come out wrong. She simply didn't want there to be any unease between them.

"I understand,'' he said after a few moments' silence, and then got to his feet.

Taken aback by his sudden move, she stared up at him.

He dusted grass and leaves off his trousers. "A sensible wish, one I am sure we can honor.'' His smile was wry. "Or at least make a valiant attempt at."

She opened her mouth, wanting to explain more clearly what she meant, but the words stuck in her throat.

He held out a hand.

She squinted at it. Did he want to pull her up? Shake on the deal? Gingerly she lifted a hand to him.

He took it in his warm palm, bowed his head and kissed the back, right above her knuckles. He smiled sadly as he straightened. "After we marry, you may stay here at the Flying Ace."

THAT EVENING, sitting on the couch in the living room, Brianna watched in simmering anger as Cord and Allie and Rafe discussed the quiet ceremony that was supposed to take place tomorrow. Everyone agreed that it would be appropriate for a justice of the peace to marry them.

Everyone except Bri. She had no intention of marrying anyone, least of all Rafe. His troubled eyes rarely met hers, as if the thought of a future with her was too painful to consider. That's why she hadn't balked about the marriage plans. Let him sweat. Tomorrow would be soon enough for her to relieve him of his warped sense of duty.

But first she'd make him get on his knees and propose properly. He hadn't asked yet, but assumed she'd be willing to marry him. And then she'd turn him down. Flatter than a pancake.

Allie was the only one excited, and Bri did feel bad about leading her on. She seemed genuinely pleased about the match, as she put it. Cord, who'd had no problem interfering in Bri's life before, seemed oddly quiet. It was inconceivable that he would go along with this ridiculous arrangement. People didn't marry just because they'd slept together.

Bri let out a pent-up breath. God, she'd actually slept with Rafe. The reminder brought heat to her cheeks and she looked down to study her hands. She was such a damn fool. Just thinking about last night got her worked up and sappy. She'd spent half the afternoon in her room, lying on her bed, replaying last night. If he asked her to go to his room right now, she'd probably race him there. How pathetic.

"Brianna? Why so quiet? Tomorrow will be your wedding day." Allie was all smiles. "You should be excited. What dress will you wear?"

The two men looked at her, one expectant, and the other wary.

Allie didn't wait for her answer. She turned to Rafe. "I almost forgot about a ring. We must find one in the morning."

Rafe nodded. He couldn't have looked less enthusiastic.

"I have my mother's ring," Cord said, studying Bri. "It's a ruby with two small diamonds."

"Brianna?" Rafe drew her attention. "Would that be all right for now? Later you may choose whatever you want."

His gaze was so unexpectedly tender, his voice low and intimate, that she started to thaw. This was the first time he'd displayed any emotion since visiting her at the lake.

"I don't need a ring," she murmured and looked back down at her hands.

After a lengthy silence, Cord got up. "I'll go get it so we can see if it fits."

"I'll help you look." Allie quickly followed him out of the room.

Bri wanted to call them both back. She didn't want to be alone with Rafe right now. The way he looked at her, the gentleness in his voice made her too vulnerable. Her mind scrambled for the anger she'd been feeling, but she found only yearning. A deep longing for him to say the marriage would be real, born of love.

"You seem troubled," he said, and moved to sit beside her on the couch.

She wanted to run. Instead, she let him take her hand. "You don't seem yourself, either."

He sighed. "There is much to do by tomorrow."

Yeah, like proposing for starters. She took a deep breath. "Rafe, we aren't getting married tomorrow."

His grip on her hand tightened, his gaze narrowed. "I do not understand."

"I know you don't," she said sadly. "Look, I'm letting you off the hook. I appreciate that you want to do the right thing, but—" She shook her head, emotion beginning to swell in her chest.

She tried to begin again, but he leaned forward and silenced her with a kiss that stole her breath away.

"Marry me, Brianna. Be my bride," he whispered against her mouth.

God help her. "Yes."

"I NOW PRONOUNCE YOU man and wife." The justice of the peace smiled benignly at them.

Bri was too nervous to respond. She just stood there, frozen, barely able to recall saying "I do."

Allie nudged Rafe. She and Cord served as witnesses. Jessica had gone back to Dallas for a couple of days and Bri wasn't sure she wanted anyone else to know yet. The idea of what she was doing was too enormous for her to absorb. Allie was already planning a big wedding back in Munir, the thought of which frightened Bri to death. She refused to think beyond today. Not that she was able. She was still too numb. And excited. She was Rafe's wife.

"Go ahead, young man," the balding justice said. "You can kiss your bride."

Holding her breath, Bri turned expectantly to Rafe. When he leaned toward her, she moved to meet him halfway, reveling in his musky male scent, the warmth of his breath on her chin. This would obviously not be too satisfying a kiss, but tonight... alone...in bed. Oh, God.

He kissed her cheek. She blinked and drew back, surprised, hurt. Her gaze darted toward the justice, who frowned at the paternal kiss. His secretary had glanced up from sealing the marriage certificate in an envelope. She looked away.

Cord cleared his throat. "We have dinner reservations at that new restaurant in Sommersville."

Rafe nodded and lightly touched the small of her back, as if she were a casual acquaintance and not his bride. "Shall we go?"

How humiliating. She wanted to scream at him, run out of the courtroom, away from pitying looks.

"Brianna?" His narrowed gaze searched her face. "Are you ready?"

She nodded, and preceded him ahead of Cord and Allie. Bri's nerves were shot. Maybe she was over-reacting. Maybe he avoided public displays of affection. Later, at home, she would be able to read him better.

As soon as they got outside, Allie faced them with troubled eyes and said, "Perhaps you two would like to dine alone tonight."

"No," Rafe said quickly. "We will all celebrate together."

Brianna didn't like the arrangements but she said nothing.

There would be plenty of time later for her and Rafe to be alone.

In fact, all through the meal Bri remained quiet. Rafe was polite and attentive. Too polite. Something was horribly wrong. Bri could hardly touch her food and wished the others would hurry. Once they were home and she was in Rafe's arms, everything would be okay.

Wouldn't it?

Allie did most of the talking, and when she started to order dessert, Bri gave her the eye. Allie got the message and declined the waiter's offer of crème brûlée.

They got back to the Flying Ace within an hour, and Cord and Allie promptly disappeared. Rafe had only one glass of champagne at dinner, but he headed straight for the scotch and poured himself a hefty portion.

"I think I may want some of that," Bri said, mostly to draw his attention.

He gave her a quizzical look. "Have you had scotch before?"

"There's always a first time for everything."

The stricken look on his face had her immediately regretting her words. He thought she was referring to the loss of her virginity. Of course she hadn't meant the remark that way. It hadn't even crossed her mind.

She laid a hand on his arm, anxious to touch more than his arm. She wanted to run her palms down his body, feel his hardness. "We've had a long day. Let's go to bed."

The misgiving she saw in his eyes stung. He took a slow sip of scotch, his eyebrows furrowed in thought. "You go ahead."

She hesitated, though maybe it wasn't such a bad idea to get a head start. Brush out her hair, undress and slip into bed before he came in.

"Okay." She moistened her lips and started down the hall, but then stopped when she remembered something. "Which room?"

He stared blankly at her.

"Yours or mine?" She shrugged, feeling shy again. "We hadn't talked about it."

He walked up to her, the unmistakable shadow of regret in his eyes, and brushed her cheek. "Go to your room, Brianna. Tomorrow morning I leave early for Dallas, and I do not wish to disturb you."

"PLEASE DON'T TALK about me like I'm not here." Bri knew Jessica and Allie were trying to help, but she was about ready to clobber both of them.

She went back to studying the instructions for the fancy new mixer she'd bought yesterday and tried to ignore their concerned stares. They'd been sitting at the kitchen table for the past half hour, refusing every hint to leave her in peace and quiet.

"Oh, God, I think she's going to bake more cookies," Jessie said with a dramatic shudder. "I can see next week's headlines in the newspaper—Serial Baker Strikes Again—local townswomen all top three hundred pounds."

Bri snorted. "Nobody is forcing you to eat them."

Allie sighed. "And we are supposed to let them sit there and stare at us? With their sad little chocolate-chip eyes pleading for attention."

Jessie made a face and put a hand to her stomach. "Don't say that. How am I supposed to eat them if I get it in my head that they're looking at me?"

Allie lifted her chin. "Perhaps I have solved your weight problem."

Jessie's eyes widened. "My what?"

"Excuse me. Potential problem."

Jessie sighed as she shook her head.

Good. Let them annoy each other for a while. They'd ganged up on Bri for the past week, trying to get her to go to a movie or out to dinner or just relax in an evening of girl talk. She wasn't interested in any of it. And she couldn't get it into their thick heads that her lack of interest had nothing to do with Rafe.

So it had been almost three weeks and he hadn't

returned from Dallas. Big deal. She hadn't expected him to. He'd made his intentions quite clear on their wedding night. He'd done his good deed by marrying her. She had his name, a bundle of cash he'd left her, so what reason did he have to return? For all she knew, he was back in Munir already.

"Ouch!" She caught her finger for the second time.

"You okay?" both women asked at once.

"Fine."

If she'd gone into town with Cord and chosen her own darn mixer instead of leaving the final decision up to her brother, she wouldn't be having so much trouble. This one was too complicated. Cord was probably paying her back for refusing to leave the house. She'd told him she wasn't feeling well, that she might be coming down with something, but he hadn't believed her.

"Want me to have a look at that?" Jessie asked.

"No," Bri said, her voice sharp as her patience stretched so thin it was ready to snap. Instead, she lost control of the mixer blade and snagged the same finger again. "Ouch. Dammit."

Jessie's eyebrows rose. "Dammit?"

"Are you all right?" Allie asked.

"I will be if you two butt out."

Allie frowned at Jessie. "What is this butt out?"

"It means she's trying to pretend that life is peachy when it really sucks, but she doesn't want her friends to help because she's as stubborn as a mule."

"Oh." Allie pursed her lips. "Then this is when it would be appropriate to say— Tough?"

Bri laughed. She couldn't help it. The two of them

would either drive her crazy or bring her out of her funk. She didn't know which she'd prefer. No, that wasn't true. What she'd prefer would be to be alone, in her room, under her covers. She hadn't lied to Cord about feeling ill. It was probably all the cookies she'd been eating instead of healthy meals. Since Rafe had gone, she'd found she didn't have much of an appetite for anything other than sweets.

A couple of good wholesome meals and she'd be herself again.

Jessie frowned. "You're awfully pale, kiddo."

"Only compared to you. I don't know what you're using on your face, but you look like a million bucks." Bri gave her the best smile she could muster. "I'm fine. Or I would be if you two buttinskies would give it a rest."

Allie's eyebrows rose questioningly at the odd word, but Jessie didn't take her gaze from Bri. "Maybe you'd feel better if you talked to him."

Bri finally shoved the blade home, which was a good thing, because if she'd failed at one more thing she would have burst into tears. "Talked to whom?"

Jessie snorted. "Who do you think?"

"I don't think. Not about him."

Allie sighed, and Bri forced herself not to respond. She felt bad for Allie. She didn't understand why Rafe had abandoned Bri, either. Or so she said.

"You know, I think this mixer is going to work out. I really like the dough attachment. I've never baked a lot of bread, but I bet I'd enjoy it."

"Brianna," Allie said gently. "You do not have to pretend. We're your friends."

Bri looked her sister-in-law in the eyes. "If you were my friends, you'd understand that I don't want to talk about Rafe. He did his duty, and now he's gone. The end."

"But—"

"Allie," Bri said, holding back hot tears of frustration. "If he had any interest, or truly wanted this marriage, he would have called. It's been three weeks, for heaven's sake. So get over it."

Allie's cheeks flushed a dusky pink as her gaze slid to Jessie. "Perhaps we should tell her."

Jessie, clearly torn, bit her lower lip.

"Tell me what?" Bri asked.

"I don't know," Jessie said to Allie, as if Bri wasn't sitting right next to her.

"It's enough," Allie went on. "It's foolishness now."

"What's foolish?" Bri stood up too quickly and the room spun for a moment. "What aren't you telling me?"

With one last meaningful glance between her two friends, Allie turned to Bri. "Rafe is at the Desert Rose. He's been there for the past week."

Her legs wobbled and she had to grab the table before she fell. Bri's insides churned with confusion and pain, and a moment later, she knew she was going to be sick. Clamping her hand over her mouth, she dashed toward the bathroom.

Allie turned back to Jessie, and the two women said nothing for a long moment while they tried not to hear Bri being sick. Finally, Jessie leaned over the table and touched Allie's hand. "Are you thinking what I'm thinking?"

"Yes. I will call him. Rafe must know."

RAFE FORCED HIMSELF to concentrate on the contract in front of him. He'd read the same paragraph five times, and he still had no clear understanding of the words. Not that the language was difficult. It was standard, from an American firm they'd done business with for years. His problem was focus.

It confused him, this obsession with Brianna. Since the day he had left, she had drawn his thoughts from every task. How he had managed to complete anything was a mystery.

He had wrongly thought each day away from her would lessen his desire to speak to her, to see her. To kiss her. Instead, she had invaded his waking moments and his dreams, as well.

It was foolish, childish. She had been very clear about her wishes that day by the lake. He still had trouble knowing he had been so wrong in his assessment of her feelings toward him. Yes, she cared about him. That, he made no mistake about. His error was in believing she wanted more.

When she had told him she wanted to pretend nothing had happened between them, he had been shocked at the depth of his disappointment. Why would he have felt such pain at her admission when he did not love her?

He sank back into his chair. He did *not* love her. Yes, he liked her very much, and yes, he missed her so much he ached for her, but that was not love.

It could not be love. He married Brianna because it was his duty. Arranged, loveless marriages were common enough, but he could not bring her to Munir. Not because of his family's disapproval, although that would be a considerable obstacle. And not because she would be inadequate in her duties as his wife. He could not bring her to his homeland because she would never be at home there.

He had done a great deal of thinking after his conversation with Cord. Brianna had been discarded by her own mother, and unwanted by her aunt. She had been an outsider in her own home. Her life had transformed when she had moved in with Cord. From what her brother had told him, she had been like a wounded filly when she first arrived, shy to the touch, fearful of being hurt again. It had taken a long time for her to belong in her world. To feel whole and necessary and entitled. How could he take her away from the only safe place she had ever known?

So it could not be love.

He stared at his paperwork, then glanced at the clock. With an hour until dinner, he had time for a ride. Thank goodness the Desert Rose had so many excellent horses. In the past week, he had ridden for hours in the early morning, and occasionally in the evening. He had also reinstated his old physical fitness regimen. One hundred push-ups before bed, twenty laps in the swimming pool. Anything and everything to keep his mind occupied. To exhaust his body. Sleep had become his most welcome friend.

He stood so quickly his chair nearly toppled. He did not give it a thought as he went to the window and pulled back the curtains. Of course the Flying Ace was not visible from here, nor the woman herself, but his imagination filled in the blanks. He remembered everything about her in agonizing detail. The silk of her cheek, the curve of her lips, the hunger in her eyes that tortured him day and night. How could she dismiss him so handily when her gaze begged him to stay? Was she so steely, so strong, that she could put into practice the firm determination to do the right thing, while he was a breath away from throwing his duty, his obligation, to the wind?

He felt as if he stood on the razor's edge. Leaving this country would be wise and prudent. Staying delayed his anguish, his uncertainty. He had his people to think of, and yet Brianna stole his thoughts. The only recourse he had was to settle things with her, assure her she would be well provided for, and then to say goodbye, go back to a life he understood.

Yes, ascending the throne would be the most difficult challenge, but he had grown up his father's son. He had a vision for his country, a noble and worthy goal.

Only, in his long hours of meditation, he had come to some startling realizations. Not about himself, but about the woman he knew some day he would marry. It was no easy task to be the wife of a sheikh. There were obligations and responsibilities most women would find taxing.

And yet, when he thought about Brianna, he could somehow see her in the role. He had watched her handle that unruly cowhand. She had a good head for business, and a clear, quick mind. Her kindness and compassion made everyone around her feel loved. Brianna could be a tremendous help in his work. She exemplified the courageous spirit of these wild Americans he had grown to admire. She wore her intelligence and dignity easily, and yet she understood what it was like to be unsure, timid. She could teach the women of Munir so much.

He had no doubts that once his family and his countrymen recovered from the shock, they would all come to love her as he did.

His hand went to the window ledge as he steadied himself. Love her? He could not love her. Had he not been perfectly clear about this point?

He sighed wearily. Yes. He had been clear. Just as he had been clear yesterday and the day before and the day before that.

Maybe, if he continued to be clear, he would come to believe it.

Enough. He admonished himself for his damn weakness. He changed his shirt, pocketed his cell phone and wallet, and headed out of his suite. He would ride until he could not think. He would ride until he could not feel.

Chapter Fifteen

Bri looked in the mirror at her straggly hair and pale face with the dark circles under her eyes. She looked like hell. Better that Rafe hadn't made an attempt to see her. Let him hide out at the Desert Rose. Who cared?

Not her.

She sniffed, and then blew her nose, loudly, until it was red. The color went so well with her sick, milky complexion. What a mess. No wonder Jessie and Allie were worried about her. And here she'd been awful to them. And to Cord, too, snapping at him left and right. But in his case, he deserved some of her foul mood. He'd chased Rafe away.

That wasn't true. Rafe had chosen to leave. He was too strong-willed to have anyone dictate his actions. The fact that he'd been staying at the Desert Rose for a week without contacting her or coming to the Flying Ace to visit Allie proved it was his wish to keep his distance from her.

And horrifyingly, everyone knew about the quickie marriage, she suddenly realized. The Colemans all had to be wondering why Rafe was staying at the Desert Rose and not here at the Flying Ace. Rumors were simmering thicker than split-pea soup by now.

Oh, God. She covered her face with her hands. How awful. How humiliating. Maybe she could go back to New Hampshire. Leave tomorrow. Cord would understand. Anyway, he had Allie now...

Someone knocked at the bathroom door and she quickly splashed some cold water on her face before answering.

"Bri, we need to talk to you." It was Jessie. "Would you come out?"

"In a minute."

"It's kind of important."

Bri dried her face and hands. She knew better than to think they'd go away if she ignored them. Much as she'd like to sneak into her room and lock the door, she knew it wouldn't be that easy. Jessie would eventually have to go home but Allie was stubborn enough to camp outside Bri's door.

"Brianna?" Allie called out this time. "You must come out. And brush your hair."

Bri frowned. Okay, now she was curious. She slowly opened the door and peeked out. Allie was right outside, but Jessie stood down the hall near the living room.

"Your hair." Allie narrowed her gaze. "Where is your brush?"

"What's going on?"

Allie glanced at Jessie. "Nothing."

"You said you wanted to talk to me...that it was important."

"We do. But you should brush your hair." Allie studied her more closely. "Powder. We need powder for your nose."

"Forget it, Allie." Jessie motioned them to hurry. "Trust me, it won't matter."

"I never knew how bossy she was," Allie whispered as she urged Bri down the hall.

"This has to do with Rafe, right?" Bri put on the brakes just before they reached Jessie. "It has to. You think I'm going over there and—"

Jessie tugged her closer and pointed toward the sliding glass doors. "Actually, we figured he might be coming here."

Rafe had already entered the courtyard. He hesitated briefly near the fountain, and then came toward the house.

"Oh my God." Bri clutched her already nervous stomach. "Oh my God."

She had no idea what to do. Run and lock herself in her bedroom? Stay and try to act casual? Yell at Jessie and Allie for springing this on her?

Both women stared at her stomach. She moved her hand away. So she was nervous. That should be no surprise to them. She tried to take a deep breath and ended up coughing when she remembered her red nose and blotched face, how hideous her hair looked.

Jessie tapped her back. "You okay?"

"No, I'm not okay. My hair and face are a mess. I look like hell."

Allie grunted. "See?"

Jessie gave her a withering look. "He won't even notice," she said, grabbing Bri's hand when she started to back away. "He wants to see you. He won't care."

"I care."

Jessie sighed. "Yeah, I know."

But it was too late. Rafe knocked at the glass door.

"I have to let him in," Allie said, her gaze uncertain as it traveled from Bri back to Rafe.

Bri nodded. Jessie was right. Rafe didn't care about how Bri looked. He didn't care about her at all.

Allie slid the door open and briefly greeted her brother before stepping back. He didn't even glance at her. His gaze went directly to Bri.

If she'd expected a smile she would've been disappointed. He stood motionless for a moment, his eyes dark with concern, his body rigid and radiating tension. So maybe he did care. Or else he was angry about something.

"Allie, how about we go make some tea?" Jessie said, and motioned for her to follow.

They promptly disappeared, leaving Bri alone with Rafe. He still hadn't said anything, but neither had she taken the initiative.

"How are you?" he asked finally, his gaze running down her body, lingering on her belly.

She glanced down self-consciously. Had she spilled something? "A little under the weather." She shrugged. "It might be a cold coming on, or a touch of the flu. You probably shouldn't get too close."

His lips curved in a wry smile.

Oh, God. She could just kick herself. What a stupid thing to say. As if he had any intention of getting close. "You want to sit down?"

Without saying anything, he moved to the couch but then waited for her to take the tan leather armchair before he sat.

"Perhaps the hot tea will be good for your stomach," he said, studying her closely as if she were some type of scientific specimen.

"My stomach? Why?"

He seemed surprised, and then a little angry. "I thought you said you were unwell."

"I am, but why—" She gasped. Surely they hadn't told Rafe she'd lost her cookies, so to speak.

He got to his feet. "What is it?"

"Nothing." She waved him to sit again. "I guess I'm not feeling that great," she mumbled, hoping he'd take the hint and leave...at the same time fearing he would.

His expression softened. Instead of returning to his seat, he came to her, his hands extended. She wasn't sure what he wanted her to do, so she tentatively put her hands out, too. He grasped them and pulled her to her feet. In seconds she was in his arms and cradled to his chest.

"I told you not to get too close," she whispered shakily. "I might be contagious."

"Ah, Brianna." He pulled away and lifted her chin until their eyes met. "You do not have to pretend."

"Pretend what?"

"I have missed you." He kissed the tip of her nose, and when she closed her eyes, he kissed each lid.

When he got to her mouth, she forgot what they were talking about. He teased her lips open and ran his tongue just inside the seam. Eagerly she opened wider for him but he continued to toy with her, nibbling her lower lip, touching it with the tip of his tongue until she thought she'd go crazy.

She whimpered when he pressed a brief kiss to her mouth and then retreated. She slowly opened her eyes. He gave her a sexy smile that made her knees weak, and then led her to the couch.

He made sure she was comfortable, grabbing an extra pillow from the other end and tucking it behind her back, and then he sat beside her.

She laughed softly. "I'm really not that sick."

His expression darkened. "You should have called me."

"I didn't know you were at the Desert Rose until an hour ago. Why didn't you call me?"

Uncertainty flickered in his eyes. "Perhaps I was wrong. I should have called."

"Wrong about what?"

"It does not matter now."

"It does to me. Do you have any idea how humiliating it is to have your new husband living a couple of miles away?"

Rafe brushed the hair away from her eyes. "No one knows about us."

Her hair. How awful it must look. Why hadn't she listened to Allie? "This is a small town. Everyone knows everything."

He gave her a patient smile, which only served to annoy her more. "Did you try to contact me?"

"How could I? I had no idea if you were still in Dallas or had gone back to Munir. Besides, *you* abandoned *me*."

"That is not true. I only wished to give you time to think and become adjusted to the idea of marriage."

"Most couples do that together." She stared down at her hand. Him showing up didn't chase the hurt away. "So, now you've decided that I've had enough time for adjustment?"

He seemed unfazed by her sarcasm. "Perhaps you have something to tell me?"

"Such as?"

His dark eyebrows drew together in a disapproving frown. "You have no news you think may be of interest to me?"

She shook her head. "Rafe, I honestly don't know what you're getting at."

"Is it safe to bring in the tea?" Allie asked as she entered the room carrying a tray. "I do not wish for anything to be thrown." Her gaze rested on them, sitting so close there was hardly space to breathe, and she grinned. "Ah, I see all is well."

Jessie followed with a plate of cookies. The sight of them nearly sent Bri running for the bathroom again. "Are you okay?" Jessie asked. "You look a little green."

"Fine." Bri put a hand to her stomach. "But if I never see another cookie again I'll be even better."

Jessie laughed. She was the only one who did. "I know what you mean. I've put away my share. And now I've got to go meet Nick and my parents for dinner." She set the plate on the coffee table. "I'll see you all tomorrow."

Bri noticed the subtle tension in the room. She just

didn't understand it. "I thought you were going back to Dallas in the morning."

"I am, but I figured I'd just check and see what happened."

Bri caught the nervous look Jessie exchanged with Allie. It made her edgy, too. "Something is supposed to happen?"

"You never know." Jessie shrugged and headed for the glass doors. "I gotta go."

"You parked in the driveway," Bri reminded her.

"I'll walk around to the back. The exercise will do me good."

Right. A fast exit was obviously what she was looking for.

"I can't stand it." Jessie stopped near the door and turned around. "I swore to myself I wouldn't do this. Not before Nick and I told Mom and Dad tonight, but I can't help it."

"What?" Bri and Allie asked in excited unison.

"Nick and I are pregnant." She put a hand on her still-flat stomach. "We're going to have a baby."

"Jessica!" Bri jumped up, nearly knocking over the tray in her haste to dole out hugs. Allie was right behind her.

Between the two of them, laughing and crying and hugging, they almost toppled Jessie to the floor. She laughed so hard she started hiccuping.

"Don't any of you dare tell my parents, or anyone that you heard about it first." Jessie dabbed at her eyes. "Keeping it to myself all day was making me a wreck." She gave Bri a watery smile. "And then when we realized you had your own little—"

"Congratulations." Rafe cupped Jessie's elbows and kissed her on both cheeks. He had stood to the side while the women had taken their turns but he'd obviously grown impatient. "May the little one add to your joy."

"Thank you." Jessie's cheeks were flushed pink, her eyes bright with excitement.

Bri felt a pang of selfish envy. She prayed it didn't show, and squeezed Jessie's hand. "Your mother is going to be ecstatic."

Jessie's smile gave way to concern. "I hope I didn't rain on your parade, Bri."

She frowned. "Why would you say that?"

Rafe slipped an arm around Bri's shoulders, momentarily stunning her into silence. "You had better go share your news," he told Jessie. "Brianna is in good hands."

"I know." Jessie grinned, dabbed at her eyes again. "I'd better go confess to Nick that I spilled the beans early. He shouldn't be too mad. He's still in shock." Laughing, she waved as she slipped out the door. Before Bri could ask her what she'd meant about raining on her parade.

She tried to catch Allie's gaze, but she had reclaimed her seat and concentrated on pouring the tea. Maybe concentrating too much. She was quiet, too, when Bri would have expected her to still be giddy over Jessie's news. It made Bri uneasy.

She pulled away from Rafe and went back to her seat and then met his watchful eyes. He didn't seem perplexed or curious about what Jessie had said, or Allie's odd behavior. It was as if they all knew something she didn't. The whole idea was maddening. She wanted to ask them what the heck was going on, but she had the weird feeling she'd dread the answer more than the not knowing.

"Cord will be coming home soon," Allie said breezily as she stood but managed to avoid Bri's warning look. "I must go see about dinner."

Now Bri knew for sure something was wrong. Allie did not volunteer to make dinner if she could get around it. "Need help?" Bri asked sweetly.

"No, thanks. Have a nice visit with my brother." She looked pointedly at Rafe. "I am assuming you will join us for dinner."

"Better find out if she's ordering pizza first," Bri whispered loud enough for Allie to hear.

"Ha! When you have made enough food for the rest of the week?" Allie called over her shoulder on her way to the kitchen.

"Oh, yeah." Of course they were having leftovers. Lord knew, Bri had cooked enough for them and the hands for a month.

Rafe frowned at her. "You look thin. You are cooking but not eating?"

That he looked genuinely concerned got her pulse racing. "I've been eating. Not always the right things."

He took one of her hands and sandwiched it between his large palms. "That must change."

The authoritative tone she could do without, but his hands were so warm and comforting, and his eyes so sincere that she forgave him. "Why are you so interested?'' she asked, half teasing, half insane with anxiety.

Rafe shook his head at her coy defense. If he had not understood women as well as he did, he might have believed her. It was a censure, a not-so-subtle punishment for not calling her, and now that he was here, he knew keeping his distance had been misguided.

The three weeks away had given him time to appreciate her in so many new ways, the least of which was that even with her hair disheveled and her nose too pink, she was still the most appealing woman he had ever seen. He wanted her now more than ever.

Perhaps being apart wasn't entirely a mistake. They had both needed time to think, to reevaluate. Although, the news of the pregnancy made him wish he could have shared the discovery with her and not hear it from Aliah and Jessie. He hated that Bri had had to go through it alone.

"Rafe? I asked you a question. Why are you so interested in my health?''

"You are my wife. I care about you.''

Her gaze shifted, a subtle move that might have been missed if one did not know her well. She didn't believe him.

"You have an odd way of showing it.''

He touched her cheek gently with his fingertips. "I am sorry if my behavior hurt you. It was not my intention. I may be well equipped to run a country, but I am still helpless before a beautiful woman.''

Bri touched her hair as her cheeks infused with pink. "I'm far from beautiful. I look terrible.''

He shook his head. "When I look at you, all I see is beauty. Beauty and strength and courage." He leaned in, kissed her gently on the lips.

She sighed and her warm breath tasted sweet on his tongue. He wanted to taste more than her breath. He wanted to know all her flavors. He wanted—

Rafe pulled back, astonished once more at her effect on him. When he was near Bri, he lost his good sense. He was not a romantic, certainly not sentimental, and yet the moment he touched her, tasted her, he became a lovesick poet.

The issues at stake were serious indeed. A country, a people, ages-old traditions would be directly impacted by his decisions about this woman.

Bri opened her eyes when he didn't kiss her again. Something was wrong. In one second he'd gone from a lover to a stranger. No wonder she wasn't feeling well. Being anywhere near Rafe would make anyone nuts. "Rafe?"

He looked at her as if he was surprised to find her there. "Yes?"

"What just happened? What's going on?"

He shook his head in that stubborn way he had.

She leaned back, slipping her hand from his tentative hold. "I don't get you at all. You disappear for three weeks, you don't even let me know you're back, and then you waltz in here as if nothing has happened. And they say women are fickle."

"Fickle?"

She nodded. "Unpredictable. Capricious. Maddening."

"But I am the most predictable man in the world.

I always do what I am supposed to do. I put my own needs aside so that I may serve my country." His dark gaze fixed on hers. "With one very obvious exception."

Keeping the connection steady, she leaned forward. "What do you want from me, Rafe?"

"I would like it very much if you would be honest with me."

"Honest?"

He nodded. "We need to be frank with each other, now more than ever."

"I'm not following you. I am honest. You're the one who has the hidden agenda."

"Nothing about me is hidden."

"Except what you want from me."

He studied her, and then abruptly rose, pacing to the other side of the room. That's when it hit her. Everyone was acting strange because they knew Rafe was leaving. Just as they'd known he was at the Desert Rose. This was goodbye.

Her stomach knotted and her heart pounded, but she didn't show it. She wouldn't show it. Rafe couldn't know how it tore her apart. Oh, God. This was it, for real. Rafe, gone forever.

"Brianna?"

"What?"

"Are you not well? Do you need some water?"

She shook her head. So much for her poker face. "I'm fine."

"Are you? Are you certain there is nothing I should know?"

"I'm not dying, if that's what you're thinking. I'm just a little under the weather, that's all."

"I did not think you were dying."

"Good. Now, why don't you tell me what you came here to say."

His head tilted slightly to the side. "We are speaking in riddles."

"I'm not."

"Very well. Let us begin again." He joined her on the couch and took her hand in his. "I understand you are displeased with my behavior and I cannot blame you. But it is no reason not to share this most wonderful moment."

Bri blinked back a rush of sudden tears. He thought saying goodbye was wonderful? Was he that glad to be rid of her?

"Brianna. I know you are carrying my child."

It took several seconds for his words to truly sink in. To realize he wasn't joking. He thought she was pregnant. Everyone— Oh, God. With Jessie's news, and Bri getting sick. This was horrible. A nightmare. "Rafe—"

"Yes?"

The speech she'd been about to deliver fell away as she realized why he'd finally come to her. Not because he loved her but because he thought she was going to have his child. It wasn't about love. Not even close to love.

"You're mistaken," she said, her voice a gruff whisper.

"No, I do not believe I am."

"Rafe, listen to me. I'm not pregnant. So you're

off the hook. You can go back to Munir with a clear conscience.''

His eyebrows came together as his gaze went to her stomach. ''I understand why you will not tell me the truth,'' he said, his voice colder than she'd ever heard it before. ''But hear this, Brianna. The child is my heir. In your country, that might not mean much, but in my country, it is everything. You *will* be my wife. And not just in name only.''

Chapter Sixteen

Bri stared in angry disbelief. "Are you asking me or ordering me?"

"You are misunderstanding my intention."

"How? Explain it."

"I promise you a good life. You and our child will have anything you want. Only the finest house and clothes and jewelry, and you can visit Cord and Aliah and your friends whenever you wish."

She swallowed back the sudden threat of tears. He didn't get it. She didn't want material things. She wanted him to love her. When she could finally trust herself to speak, she very calmly said, "I understand the importance of an heir in your country, more important to your family. I prefer to think of children as children and not heirs."

His features tightened. "You are deliberately being contrary."

"Another thing you should know…" She gave him her best patronizing smile. "In this country, women have the right to determine their own future. In this country, arrogant men and bossy big brothers don't get to have the final word. In this country, a woman gets to do whatever she damn well pleases."

"Brianna, you are completely misunderstanding me. Please calm down so we may discuss this rationally."

"You don't think I'm calm?" She tucked her hands beneath her legs so he couldn't see them shake. "That's how little you know me. I'm perfectly calm. But I am tired and I think it's time you left."

His eyes darkened. "We need to talk."

"No, you need to leave."

He stared, confused, as if he didn't know her at all. She didn't know herself right now. "Perhaps after you have rested you will be able to see reason."

She stood, afraid she'd say something she'd regret later. "Goodbye, Rafe."

"Brianna…"

She didn't wait for him to finish, but headed for her room. Just as she closed the door, she heard Allie asking for her. Bri didn't care. Let Rafe tell his sister whatever he wanted. Right now nothing mattered but getting under the covers and shutting out the world.

Bri locked her door and then crawled into bed. She snuggled under the comforter and closed her eyes. How could she be so foolish as to react this way? She knew he didn't love her. Couldn't love her even if she were sophisticated and beautiful and said all the right things. There were too many complications. She didn't belong in Munir, and he didn't belong here. Nothing had changed.

Useless tears filled her eyes and she tried in vain to blink them away. More came, spilling down her cheeks and making her so mad at herself she could scream.

If only she were pregnant, she would have an excuse to accept a marriage on his terms. Once they were married and living together, sharing the same bed, she could get him to love her. She would be the perfect wife, the perfect mother...

Punching her pillow with disgust, she muffled a sob. She really was going insane. How moronic could she get? She couldn't stay married to him, not for any reason other than love. A relationship couldn't work otherwise. She knew that.

Bri bit her lip. She couldn't go there. Wishing for his love would only make her crazy. It wasn't going to happen. His only interest in her was that he thought she carried his heir.

Soon they'd file for an annulment, he'd return to Munir, and in time she'd forget him. Life at the Flying Ace would return to normal. She'd have the ranch's bookkeeping to keep her busy and she would forget...

Oh, God, that was as much of a lie as the pregnancy. She wouldn't forget about him. Ever. How could she? Dammit, she loved him. Even his stupid little arrogant smirk when he thought he knew better. Which he didn't. Well, sometimes...but not often.

She buried her wet face in the pillow and cursed. Even if she agreed to stay married and move to Munir, it wouldn't work. It would kill her to live with him knowing he didn't love her back. Anyway, before long he'd have to believe her about not being pregnant. And then where would they be?

If only she could turn back the clock…if she had never met him… No, if she could change anything it would be that she wouldn't have seduced him…

Oh, hell. None of that mattered now. More tears rushed down her cheek as she prayed for sleep. She needed oblivion to shield her from the mess her life had become. Even if only for a night.

RAFE LAY IN BED and stared into the darkness wishing it would swallow him whole. Thoughts of Brianna and the baby would not leave his mind. He felt raw and exposed and hopelessly inept. Something was missing, yet he could not grasp the piece of the puzzle that would bring order back into his life.

Why did Brianna insist on denying the truth? She carried his child. Their child.

That was his trump card. He could persuade her to stay with him, live as husband and wife, of that he was quite sure. He need only play on her sense of fairness to their child, his or her right to live with both parents. But should he? Not just because of the obvious unpleasant manipulation involved. Her refusal had paved the way for his unencumbered return to Munir. He could leave with a clear conscience, return to his duties, to his old life.

He swore out loud. A life without Brianna. He could not imagine a happy ending to that scenario. It was not as if he could forget her. She would always be in his thoughts. In his heart.

The idea startled him. Was it not simply duty and honor that prompted his desire for a traditional marriage? Was the pregnancy merely an ideal excuse? Or was it love that made his heart pound at the sight of her? Tricked him into thinking he smelled her scent when she was not with him.

His gaze drew toward the window where the moon fought to make an appearance between the clouds. His parents would be most displeased if he were to take Brianna to Munir. Not only would they have they lost their daughter to an American husband, but they would then have to accept that their only son, the heir apparent, would not be wed to a suitable woman. That his child would have western blood.

His parents would find it difficult enough to acknowledge the union, and he could not imagine how the people of Munir would respond. Of course, he could step down, abdicate his right to the throne.

A sliver of moon escaped from the clouds. Its beam cast an eerie shadow on the wall of the suite. What the devil was he doing here in his dark silent room, driving himself insane, getting no closer to an answer? Hell, he was no longer sure of the question.

Half the moon appeared, providing enough light for a ride. Of course he knew that could change, but he threw off the coverlet, got out of bed and donned his jeans. Only a silk shirt was handy, so he jerked it on.

He had to get out in the fresh air. Go for a ride to clear his head. He hoped the stables were unlocked. Midnight. Doubtful anyone would still be around. But he had to try.

One of the Desert Rose hands, suffering from insomnia, arrived at the stables the same time Rafe did. The man unlocked the tack room and even helped Rafe saddle one of the Arabians. It had to be fate. An omen, he decided as he raced across the open pasture toward the Flying Ace.

What he hoped to find once he got there he had no idea. But he had no choice. He had to try, and perhaps fate would once again step in.

Ten minutes later, he found fate and everyone else asleep at the Flying Ace. No lights were on in the main house or the bunkhouse. He rode around to the back where the bedrooms were, but every window was dark.

Disappointment pricked him as he dismounted. He should go, keep riding toward the lake, but he stood frozen, staring at the house, as if by sheer will he could get Brianna to appear.

A light went on in the kitchen.

His heart lurched.

It was impossible to see who was in there. He tapped on the door, hoping it was Brianna.

The back porch light came on and then Aliah peered out with worried eyes that immediately widened in surprise. Quickly she opened the door.

"What are you doing out here? You scared me half to death."

He shook his head. Good question. What was he doing out here?

"Rafe? Are you all right?" She stepped out onto the porch, her gaze narrowed in concern. "Come inside."

"No, sit out here with me for a moment."

She tightened the belt of her robe and sat beside him on the top step. Placing a hand on his leg, she smiled encouragingly at him.

"She says she does not want to be my wife."

"I know." Aliah sighed. "She is as headstrong as you are."

"Has she spoken to you?"

Aliah shook her head. "She has not left her room. Cord is very worried."

"He has every right to be." Rafe briefly closed his eyes and rubbed the back of his neck. "She did not look well. I, too, am concerned."

"Why?"

He stared at her but she betrayed no emotion. What kind of question was that?

"Is it because she is carrying your child that you are concerned?"

He drew his head back in disbelief. "I am concerned for Brianna...of course for the child, as well. But Brianna is—" He cut himself off, took a deep breath.

"Yes?"

"Has she seen a doctor?"

Aliah smiled gently. "My dear brother, you think I will let you get away with changing the subject?"

"Brianna's health is the subject."

"Is it?"

He stared off into the blackness. It was a mistake coming here. His mind was too muddled, his thoughts erratic.

"Rafe?"

"I should get back." He started to stand.

She restrained him with a hand on his arm. "Why did you marry Brianna?"

"You ask such a ridiculous question? You are the

one who reminded me of my duty, and then revealed that she is carrying my child.''

''Was that the only reason?''

He hesitated. ''Why else? You are the only one here who understands what obstacles we would face. Our parents, the citizens, will all have strong opinions regarding a western queen. Our enemies would look to use the union to their advantage.''

''Ah, Rafe, you fool yourself. Our allies have confidence in your strengths and vision. They will not be persuaded otherwise because of your choice of bride.''

He did not respond except to squeeze her hand. Some sensitive matters Aliah did not understand.

Or was she right? Did he fool himself?

''I am still awaiting my answer,'' she said patiently, and when he lifted a questioning eyebrow, she added, ''Why did you marry Brianna?''

All the fight left him. He no longer had the strength for a denial. ''I love her.''

Aliah nodded, a pleased curve to her mouth. ''What will you do about your feelings?''

''I have no idea.''

''Men.'' She sighed and shook her head. ''My dear brother, the answer is simple. You must tell Brianna, of course, and then make her believe you.''

Rafe laughed without humor. ''Simple?''

BRI BRUSHED HER TEETH twice, once to make up for last night, and then brushed out her hair. No easy task. Crying had depleted her enough to fall asleep, but her night had obviously been restless judging by the amount of tangles she encountered.

The house seemed eerily quiet as she trudged down the hall toward the kitchen. She wouldn't mind one bit if Cord and Allie weren't here. She knew she had to face them sooner or later, but later sounded awfully good. But someone had to be home because she smelled coffee, which she wasn't sure excited her or made her nauseous.

Before she got to the kitchen, out of the corner of her eyes, she saw movement in the dining room. Seldom did anyone use that room. She ducked her head inside and saw that the table was set, complete with flowers.

"Ah, you are awake." Rafe came into view, dressed casually in jeans and a white shirt with the sleeves rolled back, a pitcher of water in his hand. He set it aside on the buffet and pulled out a chair. "Please, sit."

Her hand went to her hair. Thank God she'd brushed it. "What are you doing here?"

"Making you breakfast. Aliah explained how you like your eggs." A sheepish expression crossed his face. "Unfortunately, I do not have the art of omelette making perfected yet. However, I believe I have toasted your English muffin exactly to your taste."

Bri's gaze went back to the table. He had used Cord's mother's good silver. This was unreal. "Where are Cord and Allie?"

"They went to Bridle."

"We're alone?"

His left eyebrow went up in amusement. "I believe I saw Mittens hiding behind the couch."

"Very funny." She ran her clammy palms down her jeans. At least they weren't the worst pair she owned. "Thank you for going to the trouble, but I'm not really hungry."

"Aliah said you ate nothing last night."

"Aliah talks too much."

He smiled and poured a cup of coffee from the carafe he had sitting on the buffet warming tray, and then set it on the table. "Please sit with me."

She wanted to run. All the way to the lake without stopping. How could he expect her to sit and have a normal conversation? How could she pretend that just looking at him didn't break her heart? "I don't think it's a good idea."

"Please."

She crossed her arms over her chest, hugging herself as she slowly slid onto the chair he indicated.

"Thank you." He moved the cup of coffee closer to her. "You take cream with this, yes?"

She nodded. "When are you leaving for Munir?" She sounded horribly abrupt, but she didn't care. The sooner he was gone the better.

"That depends." He poured a small amount of cream into her coffee, stopping as soon as she put her hand up.

"On what?"

"How long it takes to convince you to go with me."

Darn good thing she hadn't taken a sip yet. She

sputtered anyway. "I'm not going anywhere with you."

He shrugged. "Then perhaps I should start looking for a nearby ranch to purchase."

She stared blankly at him. "What are you saying?" Her breath caught painfully in her chest. "Why are you doing this?"

"I cannot have my wife living on another continent."

Her foolish heart leaped. "You were quite willing to do that a few weeks ago."

"I was a fool."

She looked down at her hands curled into fists and said nothing. She didn't know what to say, how to respond to this cruel game he played.

"Brianna?" When she wouldn't look up, he asked, "Do you believe that I asked for your hand out of obligation and duty?"

Did he really expect an answer? Oh, God, why couldn't she just disappear? Why couldn't he have left for Munir already?

When she still refused to look at him, he lifted her chin and forced her to meet his eyes. "What would you say if I told you that I want you for my queen, whether or not you are pregnant?"

His earnest gaze never wavered and hope began to grow in her heart. She swallowed, and tried to think of something to say, but words failed her.

He dragged a chair closer to her, sat in it and then took both her hands. "I will not lie, we will have many obstacles to face. My parents will not be pleased at first. They will not welcome you with open arms. I will receive criticism from the media and po-litical opponents. Some will shun you. Their actions will be subtle, but you will know and it will hurt.''

Bri let out a ragged breath, along with the short-lived hope she'd harbored. How much longer could she go on being so darn foolish? He didn't want her. How much more discouragement did he think she needed?

"At times it will be lonely for you, but you will always be free to travel with me or come back to visit your family. You will have—''

"Rafe.'' She put a hand to his mouth to stop him and then jerked away from the intimacy. "It's okay. You don't need to explain. I know it can't work be-tween us. You have a duty to your country. I respect your loyalty.'' She smiled sadly. "Go back to Mu-nir.''

His totally bewildered look gave her pause. "You would not be willing to try?''

"I'm saying that you don't have to feel responsible for me. Leave with a clear conscience. I'll never blame you. We made no promises. An annulment will be quick and easy.'' Her words and thoughts di-verged. Maybe he wasn't trying to discourage her. Maybe he simply wanted to make her aware of the challenges they'd face. Together.

"Brianna, I think you misunderstand.'' His grip of her hands was almost heartbreakingly desperate.

"Maybe so.'' She stopped him when he started to speak but continued to hold his gaze steady. "I have to say something important. I'm not pregnant.''

He studied her face for an eternal moment, myriad

emotions swirling in his eyes. "I think I already knew that. I wanted to believe you were pregnant for my own selfish reasons." His self-mocking smile touched her. "If you carried my child, I would have no choice but to stay married to you. Everyone would understand. I am a coward."

"Oh, Rafe, no, you aren't..."

This time he silenced her with a finger to her lips. "I am a coward. A selfish one. I love you, Brianna, and I cannot bear to think of a future without you. Even given all the challenges I know we will face. How at times it will take every ounce of your courage. And mine. I know all this and still I cannot let you go."

Oh, God, she was going to cry. She bit her lower lip, blinked as fast as she could. The tears couldn't be stopped.

He kissed the back of her hands. "As difficult as life in my country can be, I will make it up to you in many, many ways. I will never take you for granted, or let my duties keep me away from you. You will share the throne and give your opinions freely. I will seek your counsel. You will make me a better ruler. You already make me a better man."

Bri swallowed and her breath shuddered in her chest. Darn it, she couldn't speak. She couldn't even tell him yes. That she wanted to be his wife. That she would gladly bear his children. That she would willingly go anywhere he'd take her.

"Brianna." He touched her wet cheek, concern in his eyes. "Are these happy tears?"

She nodded, and took his hand. When she got up,

he stood with her, and then followed as she led him down the hall to her bedroom. She locked the door behind them, and then faced him while she unbuttoned her blouse.

His curious gaze roamed her face and then rested on her hands. "What are you doing?"

"I was thinking…" She moistened her lips. "It's not too late to make that baby."

"Brianna." He stilled her hands. "This is not about a child or an heir or anything except my love for you."

"I know." She kissed him gently on the lips while she disengaged his hands. "I love you with all my heart. And I'm going to be the best darn sheikh's wife you ever saw. But first, we're going to make love. Right here. Right now."

She unfastened her last two buttons and then slid the blouse off her shoulders. "I have a feeling that as soon as we tell Cord and Allie, our lives are going to get a little hectic."

She held her breath and resisted the urge to shut her eyes as he unclasped the front of her bra. He pushed the cups aside and looked at her with such worshipful longing her heart nearly exploded.

"You see? This is the perfect example of why you will be a most extraordinary queen."

"My breasts?"

He laughed softly. "No. Because your logic is impeccable, your timing exquisite, and your wisdom…" His gaze stayed on her breasts as he cupped one and then the other. "Brianna, together, we will change history."

His fingers did magical things to her nipples. "Uh, can we change history later?"

He smiled and lowered his head, stopping briefly to kiss her lips, and then touching her nipple with his tongue. He knelt before her, unzipped her jeans and pulled them down her thighs. He then cupped her hips, steadying her while she stepped out of the denim.

When he kissed the soft skin of her belly, her breath shuddered. When he took the elastic of her panties between his teeth and started to draw then down, her knees buckled.

He caught her and lifted her onto the bed. In seconds he'd discarded his shirt and jeans and stretched out beside her. "I love you, Brianna," he whispered, "I want to make you my wife in every sense. You have me forever."

Bri had never wanted anything more in her life. She couldn't have dreamed up a better ending.

Epilogue

Bri thought she'd be nervous. She was a little, but not enough that it showed. Or so Jessie and Allie claimed.

They both stood to the left of her in front of the altar, along with Hannah Coleman and Livy Asad Al Farid. Livy lived in the neighboring country of Balahar and had come to see Bri soon after she and Rafe had arrived in Munir. Bri hadn't known Livy that well when she worked as a ranch hand at the Desert Rose. Shortly after Bri had moved to Bridle, Livy married Sharif Asad Al Farid, Alex, Cade and Mac Coleman's newly-found brother. He'd gone to the Desert Rose to meet his brothers for the first time and he and Livy had a whirlwind, fairy-tale romance. After their marriage, Livy returned to Balahar with him where he ascended the throne and became the new ruling Sheikh. Livy had forged the way for Bri. She'd become a fast and valued friend in the past three weeks, warning Bri of the possible pitfalls that were a by-product of the different cultures and saving her from more than one faux pas.

Not that Rafe would have cared if Bri had made a

hundred mistakes. She had never felt more adored and cherished in her entire life. Spoiled rotten and loving it. Although she still wasn't accustomed to having so many servants attending to her needs.

She honestly didn't have much for them to do, and at first, the three women who were assigned to assist her seemed concerned, probably fearing for their positions in the palace. But Bri found several charities that interested her and she and the three women would have their hands full for the next decade.

"Look who just walked in," Livy whispered with a smile directed at the temple door.

King Zak and Queen Rose of Balahar, Livy's in-laws had just entered. A newlywed herself, Queen Rose looked radiant in a peach linen suit. That so many people likened Bri to the elegant woman pleased her greatly. She wanted to look that beautiful and sophisticated someday.

"I wonder where my husband is." Livy squinted at the door. "Shay is supposed to be with them."

"I saw him with Mac and Cade a few minutes ago." Hannah motioned with a jut of her chin. "There he is in the corner with Rafe."

Bri's gaze flew in that direction. The temple was so packed she hadn't even seen him enter. The people of Munir had lined up hours before the ceremony was to begin, all hoping for a spectator's seat. It seemed impossible that they had accepted her so quickly. Even Rafe had been surprised. His mother, who had an amazingly wonderful sense of humor, joked that they were relieved that Rafe had finally married.

The music started and the murmurs quieted while Bri kept her eyes trained on her husband. The ceremony was a formality to appease the citizens. Of course, Rafe's parents hadn't been thrilled that they'd missed the exchange of vows of their only son, either. That there would be another celebration had never been a question. Bri had kept her mouth shut and gone with the flow.

Rafe, along with Cord and Mac Coleman, started down the aisle toward her. She took a deep breath, mindful of the snugness of the white satin-and-lace gown. It was the most incredible work of art with over a thousand pearls sewn in. Bri had nearly fainted at the cost, but Rafe promised her the gown would somehow be parlayed into funds for her adopted charities.

He had promised to make her happy. She had already received a greater gift from him. Peace and acceptance. It didn't matter that her nose was crooked or that she did not come from royal lineage. He loved her just as she was, flaws and all. And she loved him, enough to tackle a new culture, a new way of life...sometimes the idea scared her senseless, but Rafe was always there beside her with a strong arm around her shoulders and whispered words of love that she felt to her very core.

Rafe approached, and Bri gave him all her attention. His sexy smile still had the power to make her knees weak and she gladly accepted Jessica's arm for support. Interesting that it was Munir's custom that the groom came to the bride. Ironic, too, because Brianna would have followed her husband anywhere. And in her heart of hearts, she knew for her, he would walk to the ends of the earth.

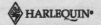

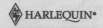

Coming in August...

UNBREAKABLE BONDS

by

Judy Christenberry

Identical twin brothers separated at birth. One had every opportunity imaginable. One had nothing, except the ties of blood. Now fate brings them back together as part of the Randall family, where they are thrown into a maelstrom of divided loyalties, unexpected revelations and the knowledge that some bonds are simply unbreakable.

Dive into a new chapter of the bestselling series *Brides for Brothers* with this unforgettable story.

Available August 2002 wherever paperbacks are sold.

HARLEQUIN®
Makes any time special ®

Visit us at www.eHarlequin.com

PHUB-R

Princes...Princesses...
London Castles...New York Mansions...
To live the life of a royal!

In 2002, Harlequin Books lets you escape to a
world of royalty with these royally themed titles:

Temptation:
January 2002—*A Prince of a Guy* (#861)
February 2002—*A Noble Pursuit* (#865)

American Romance:
The Carradignes: American Royalty (Editorially linked series)
March 2002—*The Improperly Pregnant Princess* (#913)
April 2002—*The Unlawfully Wedded Princess* (#917)
May 2002—*The Simply Scandalous Princess* (#921)
November 2002—*The Inconveniently Engaged Prince* (#945)

Intrigue:
The Carradignes: A Royal Mystery (Editorially linked series)
June 2002—*The Duke's Covert Mission* (#666)

Chicago Confidential
September 2002—*Prince Under Cover* (#678)

The Crown Affair
October 2002—*Royal Target* (#682)
November 2002—*Royal Ransom* (#686)
December 2002—*Royal Pursuit* (#690)

Harlequin Romance:
June 2002—*His Majesty's Marriage* (#3703)
July 2002—*The Prince's Proposal* (#3709)

Harlequin Presents:
August 2002—*Society Weddings* (#2268)
September 2002—*The Prince's Pleasure* (#2274)

Duets:
September 2002—*Once Upon a Tiara/Henry Ever After* (#83)
October 2002—*Natalia's Story/Andrea's Story* (#85)

Celebrate a year of royalty with
Harlequin Books!
Available at your favorite retail outlet.

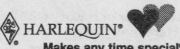